AFTERNOON DELIGHT

Also by Alison Tyler

AFTERNOON DELIGHT

EROTICA FOR COUPLES

EDITED BY
ALISON TYLER

CLEIS
PRESS

Published in the United States by Cleis Press Inc., P.O. Box 14697, San Francisco, California 94114.

Printed in the United States.
Cover design: Scott Idleman
Cover photograph: Eryk Fitkau/Getty Images
Text design: Frank Wiedemann
Cleis Press logo art: Juana Alicia
First Edition.
10 9 8 7 6 5 4 3 2

"Forbidden Fruit" by Ric Amadeus originally appeared in *Juicy Erotica* (Pretty Things Press, 2003). "View of a Room" by Jason McFadden originally appeared in *Penthouse Variations* (December, 2006). "Night Shift" by Rita Winchester originally appeared in *Frenzy* (Cleis Press, 2008).

For SAM

Summer afternoon—Summer afternoon...the two most beautiful words in the English language.
—Henry James

There was a disturbance in my heart, a voice that spoke there and said, I want, I want, I want! It happened every afternoon, and when I tried to suppress it it got even stronger.
—Saul Bellow

Contents

| INTRODUCTION

Imagine twenty-four hours of sex—from an early morning wake-up call, through midafternoon quickies, to late evening romps. The stars fade. The hot white light of dawn appears. Time for a new day and a new way to play.

Rachel Kramer Bussel's "Early Birds" are ready to go before sunrise:

> When our neighbors first decided to have construction workers come and drill loudly every morning starting at six, I was ready to murder them. I'm not by any stretch of the imagination a morning person. Even after my first two cups of Earl Grey tea, I'm still what you might call slightly sullen—or what my husband Perry might call grouchy. At least, I was, until Perry found a way to ensure that morning is my favorite time of the day.

Andrea Dale serves up "Breakfast in Bed" of the bondage variety:

*Delicious aromas tickled my nose. Aw, he'd brought
me breakfast in bed! Before I even opened my eyes, I
started to sit up.*

*That's when I discovered that he'd also managed
to tie my hands to the brass headboard.*

A collection of panties—and the memories each pair calls up—
forms the basis for rocking afternoon sex in Sophia Valenti's
"Chloe's Confession":

*There were so many pairs scattered about, I could
walk across the room and never actually have my feet
touch her hardwood floor. There were cotton boy-
shorts, lacy thongs, satin briefs—far too many to
count. I bent down and picked up a pair of ruby red
silk string bikinis from a nearby pile. As I toyed with
the slick material, it felt like water slipping through
my fingers. My cock twitched in recognition as I lost
myself in the mental image of the garment stretched
tightly across her sleek, shaved mound.*

N. T. Morley's "Black Light" uses neon paint and 1970s-era
lighting to illuminate a couple's late-evening phosphorescent sex
life:

*"And everyone can see," Mike said into her ear, his
thumb working her clit.*

*It took her a moment to realize what he'd said; by
then, he had slid three fingers into her, out, in again,
then out; she'd already undone his belt buckle and
had his cock out and was about to bend forward to
take it in her mouth. She was moments from his cock*

and both of them smeared with paint, when it dawned on her what he'd just said.

"What?"

He looked puzzled. "Everyone can see," he said. "You were watching."

With one orange-glowing hand, he gestured over to the webcam propped on a tripod, pointing right at them.

From predawn pounding to late-night lust, *Afternoon Delight* is filled with sex 'round the clock. Are you ready for your wake-up call?

XXX,
Alison Tyler

AFTER MIDNIGHT

Nikki Magennis

Come to me, baby. No, don't turn on the light. Feel your way across the room. Careful. Watch your feet. Follow the sound of my voice. You know where I am—where I always am at this hour. Sitting in the window, letting the blue night chill my skin.

I love the small hours. Silence, stillness. Out of the blackness, your slow breath, the sudden warmth of your touch. Fingertips counting down my spine and reaching into the shadows, seeking out the hot spots. Spreading me out naked in front of the window—it's enough to make the moon blush.

EARLY BIRDS

Rachel Kramer Bussel

When our neighbors first decided to have construction workers come and drill loudly every morning starting at six, I was ready to murder them. I'm not by any stretch of the imagination a morning person. Even after my first two cups of Earl Grey tea, I'm still what you might call slightly sullen—or what my husband Perry might call grouchy. At least I was, until Perry found a way to ensure that morning is my favorite time of the day.

We end almost every night together with some form of sex. If we're super horny, we'll go at it like rabbits, doing it once, then waiting a little while, then doing it again (one of the benefits of being partnered with a younger man is that at twenty-seven, Perry can pretty much go all night, while I, on the cusp of forty, am just hitting my sexual peak). But in the mornings, I used to prefer blankets over blow jobs. I'd feel his erection pressing against me, and slide away from him. It wasn't that I didn't lust after him, I just didn't think I could get it together enough to offer up the proper enthusiasm for the act, and if you're not gonna be into it one hundred percent, why bother?

But the drilling must have lit a spark in Perry's mind, because one day, it wasn't his cock I felt on me, but his tongue. There. Yes, right there between my legs. He'd kissed his way lightly along my hips, then down my thighs before parting them. I felt his sexy stubble brushing against my delicate inner thighs, that area I used to be so embarrassed about, with its pale, soft wiggliness. But Perry loved to linger there, nipping at my skin, teasing me with light brushes of his tongue along my sex. And that's exactly what he did as the drilling played outside. Just when I started to buck up against him, though, he did something even more amazing: Perry slipped his fancy, expensive headphones over my head.

Immediately, the drilling was no more, and in its place was Portishead, music to fuck by if ever there was. Or rather, in this case, music to get head by. I was awake yet relaxed, with two huge, fluffy pillows behind me, allowing me to watch as my hot young hunk slowly slurped his way to my center. He kept looking up at me for approval, his wicked, boyish grin making me melt. I spread my legs wider, letting them drop down to give him better access.

Before Perry, I thought I was so sexually sophisticated. I'd bedded more guys than I could even remember—though all the women I'd seduced stuck out in my head loud and clear. There were only a handful, but they were memorable, and I thought of their heavy breasts, spankable asses, pretty lips, and wet, open pussies when I masturbated. Some of the guys were memorable, too, like the one who'd fucked me on top of his car, or the one who'd given me my first rabbit vibrator.

But there was one act I had never really been able to let go about, and that was getting head. Sure, I got regular bikini waxes. I was in touch with my body, stroking my pussy every night, using all kinds of vibrators. I loved my cunt; I just didn't love being on the receiving end of a tongue. I felt antsy, anxious while it was happening, like it was something to get over and done with, not a sensual feast in and of itself.

I don't know if Perry had been with girls like me before, or simply intuited what he had to do, but he never pushed. He accepted my refusal of head as calmly as he accepted that I wouldn't fly overseas and didn't like shrimp, no matter how many times he taunted me with cocktail sauce. I'm a stubborn girl, and that's part of my charm. I had figured we were over the oral sex battle, as I'd dubbed it in my head after one too many exes had practically forced their mouths on me.

But Perry was sly. He made sure he had me hook, line and sinker, and the night we got engaged, once he had that gorgeous amethyst glinting on my ring finger (we're nothing if not untraditional), he started telling me about his ex, Maya. Maya was The One Who Got Away, and, I'd always be jealous of her. I told him that I'd marry him as long as he finally spilled the beans about her. And so he did, giving me everything I'd wanted to know and more about their three-year relationship, including the fact that she'd demanded to have her pussy licked every day. Yes, even when she had her period. Even when she had a cold. Even while they went camping.

"I thought I knew a lot about women and how to please them before that, but Maya showed me so much. She made me really love the taste of pussy, and not just the taste, but the feel, the shape, the force behind a woman. I ate her out in so many different positions and places. She made it hot for me, made me crave doing it. She showed me how versatile an act cunnilingus can be." He signed contentedly, and I looked down and saw that his cock was hard. Rock hard. Sticking straight up. Was I jealous? Well, Maya was the one who had run off with a fashion designer and left him crying into his bowl of Wheaties (literally, that's what he was eating when she broke up with him). And I was here.

But, okay, yes, I was a little jealous. I'd be letting this Maya bitch get away with being the one who was most prominent on his tongue if I never let Perry go down on me. So it was pure, seething jealousy, I'm a bit ashamed to admit, that finally got me over the getting-head hurdle. I told Perry he could try, but not to expect miracles, or waterfalls. I wasn't a gusher; I wasn't the type to climax from his mouth alone.

Or so I thought. "Climb on top of me," he said, indicating his mouth. He wanted me to straddle his face. That was the most embarrassing of all the oral sex positions. "Really?" I asked, stalling.

"Yes, really."

And so I did. I clutched the headboard and held on for dear life. Perry took his time, running his tongue along my lips, letting me get used to the sensation. You can probably guess what happened—after about half an hour, a good twenty-five minutes longer than I'd ever let cunnilingus continue, I came, and boy, did I come! I came all over his mouth, his chin, his neck. I exploded, from the inside out. I dug my nails into the wood of the headboard. I was hooked.

As Portishead unwound into my eardrums, I reveled in another glorious orgasm thanks to Perry's tongue. He went on, sucking my clit, swirling his tongue in just the right way, adding his fingers into the mix, until I did it again. I probably made noise when I came, but with the headphones on, I didn't hear.

He slipped them off and whispered, "Your turn," in my ear. He was naked, and his cock beckoned to me. And in case you're wondering, it's not a one-sided deal. I love giving head. The drilling was still going on but suddenly I didn't care. I lunged for his cock, my body primed from my previous orgasms. Sometimes I think I'm a real-life incarnation of Linda Lovelace's famous film role. When I get aroused, I want something in my mouth. Wait, scratch that—I want Perry's cock in my mouth. Anything else is just a poor substitute. So after I'd come, being able to suck him in all his hard, aching glory, was like whipped cream on top of a banana split. I opened my mouth and ran the head of his circumcised cock against my tongue. He reached for the headphones and put them on himself this time, and as the sun sliced through the window, I swallowed his nine-inch hard-on, and my pussy responded in kind, acting like it hadn't just been treated to his tongue's tender loving care.

No, my pussy demanded to be in on this action, so with one hand wrapped around his wet, slippery cock, I reached below with the other and began diddling my cunt. I looked up, saw Perry's eyes on me, and knew he was taking it all in—my mouth tight around him, my frantic breathing, my searching fingers. He, like me, couldn't enjoy getting head unless the giver was turned on as well. We're a perfect match like that. I took him all the way down, just the way he likes, and shoved four fingers inside myself. I moaned, and tried to say, "Oh, yeah," but the words just hummed against his shaft. His hands had been behind his head, the picture of leisure, but then he moved to stroke my hair, mussing it. He likes to see me messy and wild as I suck him. I turned my head from side to side, tears of joy filling my eyes as I moved faster, rocking my hips in time to my mouth.

I let go again, in a different kind of way, the buzzing of our arousal drowning out any noise coming in from outdoors. "Hmm," I practically screamed, but again, a scream that was muffled by the hard dick in my mouth.

"Yeah, baby," he said softly, plunging his hands into my hair, that pressure just right as I kept going. He stroked my cheek, then my neck, then shifted so he could sit up slightly and pinch my nipple. I moaned and effortlessly deep-throated his entire cock, keeping my lips pressed against his pubic hair as long as I could before rising upward. "Come on my face," I blurted after sucking in a few breaths.

He held his cock and I rubbed it against my cheeks, my lips, my neck, wanting to get as much of it in me, on me, as I could to make it a part of me. Perry slowly pumped up and down—he's not one to jerk himself crazy fast. I watched as his dick emerged from his hand, swollen and stretched so tight. I stuck out my tongue and used the flat width of it to lick his crown, then turned the pointed tip to touch his sweetest spot. Then I sucked just the head, while he squeezed and pumped. My breath was escaping in trembling gasps, my cunt tight around my fingers, when I felt the first hot spurt of his warm cream. I stilled my hand inside me and focused on the feel of the facial, the sensual bath of lust that he was giving me. I'm so honored that Perry wants to coat me like this, to grant me his delicious semen. He spattered me till there was none left, then kissed me lustily, smearing his juices all around. Then we got in the shower for some steamy, slippery fucking.

That's how I came to be a first-thing-in-the-morning blow job queen, a role that has continued even after our neighbors' construction ended. Is our morning oral wake-up call better than our nighttime fucking, or our afternoon quickies, or our postwork sex sessions, or my "emergency" solo time with my vibrator under my desk at work? It's hard to say. I like it all. I can tell you that getting and giving head right along with the sunrise is the perfect start to my morning. If you knew Perry, you'd understand.

BREAKFAST IN BED

Andrea Dale

Believe me, it was one of *those* good dreams. You know, the kind you just don't want to end. It doesn't even involve specific details, or flying, or the next day's lottery numbers.

It involves sweaty limbs sliding across sweaty limbs, skin aflame with a thousand sensations, and a pleasurable throbbing pressure between your legs that intensifies, and you don't have to do anything, just revel in the sensations of the orgasm that's coming any second now....

The kind of dream that always—*always*, dammit—gets interrupted.

As we lay spooned together, I felt my husband's breath on the back of my neck, then a series of light, playful kisses at the nape. Struggling up through the layers of sleep, I murmured a protest.

"The kids are at your mother's, remember?" he said, nibbling on my earlobe.

Right. I stifled a yawn, still unwilling to reach full wakefulness if I didn't absolutely have to respond to a crisis. It took me another moment to fully comprehend that Cal was feeling frisky and intent on taking full advantage of the fact that we would not be interrupted by a pair of small, shrieking pajama-clad bodies who would fling themselves onto the bed and demand Count Chocula and the DVD of *Shrek 2* for the billionth time.

I'd already gotten started in my dream, and I tried to recapture the sensations, the level of arousal. But as all dreams do, this one was already fading, skittering away as if burned by the morning sun.

I snuggled back against Cal. His half-hard cock pressed into the crack of my ass, and it twitched in response to my encouraging wiggles.

Cal stroked my hip, moved his hand to my breast and caressed my nipple, lightly pinching. Thirteen years of marriage, and he knew what I liked.

Problem was, it was too much knowledge. Too much comfort. "Button-pushing," a friend of mine had called it. At the time I'd thought she was jaded, but now I understood what she was trying to say. Cal knew my body, knew how I reacted. Push this button, push that button, entry, completion. A few kisses, a few minutes of medium-grade nipple play, hands or tongue ensuring I was wet enough, then intercourse, which included one orgasm of mine before he came. A few final minutes of cuddling, and then time to put on a robe and check on the kids and pack lunches for the next day and maybe pay a bill or two before collapsing in exhaustion.

I'm not saying it wasn't fun. I'm saying it was tipping the scales toward boredom.

We were too familiar with each other, too knowledgeable about each other's likes and dislikes. There was nothing else to learn or explore.

Now there would be no distractions, though, and the dream

remnants helped the mood. A delicious ache built again in my cunt, swelling my pussy lips. On schedule, Cal dipped his hand between my thighs. I spread my legs to give him better access. I gasped when his fingers slid across my clit.

"Wow, you're so wet this morning," he murmured.

I tried to turn over, to change the routine, but he was already sliding inside me, his wide cock a pleasurable fit, stretching and filling me.

He set up a steady rhythm. His breath puffed by my ear in time with his strokes. The pleasure built again, as it had in the dream, as he rubbed against my G-spot. Still, in this position, he never got quite deep enough to tip me over the edge. His hand between my legs helped fill in the blanks.

But the steady caresses on my clit changed to irregular ones as he got closer to his own orgasm. My free hand fluttered as if of its own accord, and I vaguely tried to decide if I should play with my own nipples or push his hand away and help myself, but then he let out a long, low groan and made a series of short, jerking thrusts that signaled his release.

Um. Wow. I couldn't remember the last time he'd come before making sure I'd come. I started to say something, but after thirteen years of marriage, it was still difficult. I didn't want to hurt his feelings. If there was a gracious way to destroy a man's afterglow by announcing you hadn't come yet...well, I didn't know what it was.

He kissed my shoulder in a contented, loving, but nonsexy kind of way, and slipped out of me. I bit back a sigh. I started to throw back the covers, but he caught them in his hand.

"Enjoy a quiet morning without the kids," he said. "I'll throw something together for breakfast."

Through heavily lidded eyes, I watched him bend over to pick up a pair of shorts. Sturdily built, of Scottish descent, he had a great pair of thighs, muscular and dusted with blond hair, and curving up at the top to join with his fine, tight ass. He pulled up the shorts, blocking my view of his butt, and turned to blow me a kiss.

I smiled and snuggled deeper into the cocoon of pillows and blankets. I didn't even bother to get up and go to the bathroom to clean up. I always laundered the bedding on Saturday anyway...

I must have been backlogged on needing sleep, because I didn't fall back into the dream, even though I'd hoped to. Nope, I slid right down into the total blackness of exhaustion.

I knew this because, when I slowly ascended through layers of consciousness, I discovered Cal had been very busy and I'd slept right through all of it.

Delicious aromas tickled my nose. Aw, he'd brought me breakfast in bed! Before I even opened my eyes, I started to sit up.

That's when I discovered that he'd also managed to tie my hands to the brass headboard.

Even when we were younger, pre-kids, we hadn't been terribly experimental. Oh, the occasional public quickie in a parked car, once in a while in the shower, that sort of thing. But over the years we'd settled on three or four standard positions, with oral sex every other encounter and a full-on oral orgasm for birthdays. The last few years we hadn't even been able to get away for our anniversary. The fact that the kids were spending last night and most of today away was a rare luxury.

And I'd already been mentally filling my day with the type of housework that was hard to do with active little ones underfoot.

Sad.

Not so sad now, though. Panic skittered through me, but I also trusted Cal completely, so I didn't entirely lose it. When my eyes flew open, he was standing right there, smiling reassuringly, and I immediately knew that if I asked him, he'd untie me.

"I realized," he said, "that's it's been far too long since I brought you breakfast in bed." He set the tray down on the bedside table. Tantalizing aromas wafted over the air, almost visible, like the floaty cloud-fingers they have in cartoons to indicate strong smells.

Good lord, I really did need to get out more. I was thinking in cartoon metaphor.

My stomach rumbled, the sound not unlike what would be heard in a cartoon to indicate hunger. I was doomed.

But I wasn't going to go hungry for long.

I couldn't see the entire tray, but what I could make out looked delectable: Narrow slices of honeydew melon. Strawberries and a small pot of whipped cream. Paper-thin crêpes, golden-brown.

"It's going to be a little hard for me to eat without my hands," I pointed out.

Cal chuckled. "It was the only way I could think of to make sure you enjoyed your breakfast, rather than bolting it down on your way to make the shopping list."

Damn, but he had me pegged. The idea of being tied up wasn't bothering me—no, what really gnawed at me was the fact that I had Things to Do. Normally I'd eat a bagel in front of the computer while I paid bills and sip coffee while doing the dishes or chopping vegetables for the Crock-Pot.

Beneath it all, there was a tiny frisson of disappointment. This wasn't about sex after all. I completely appreciated what he was doing, especially since he was right about me not taking the time to enjoy meals. But it had been a nice thought, for the few moments that it had lasted, that the button-pushing monotony might be superseded by something more imaginative.

Oh, well. What I could see of breakfast looked pretty amazing, and it all smelled even better. Was that French vanilla blend? Didn't we save that for guests?

Cal smeared a crêpe with cream cheese, topped it with a ruby red jam, and deftly rolled it into a skinny tube. I obediently opened my mouth. The faster we got this over with, the faster I could get up and...

...Oh. Oh, that was good. He fed the end into my mouth, and when I bit down, the savory cheese and sweet jam oozed onto my tongue. Cal continued to feed it to me in small sections, and I delighted in every morsel.

Something about the inability to feed myself, or maybe about being fed, acted like a drug on my brain. I felt myself relax, accept, slip into the moment. All that mattered was the next morsel and how it would taste.

Cal held a slice of ripe, sweet melon to my lips. The juices dribbled down my chin, tickling as they dripped down my neck. I flicked the corners of my mouth clean. I was helpless to clean up the rest of it, and there was something entirely decadent about letting the sticky-sweet juices dry on my skin, like I was a tanned, bare-breasted native girl, not-quite-innocent, draped with fragrant, bright-hued flowers, dancing for the famous explorer.

Wow, where had *that* image come from? What had Cal put in the food, anyway?

"Aren't you eating?" I asked.

I don't think I'd ever seen such a wickedly sly smile on Cal's face....

"I thought you'd never ask."

He leaned over me; I expected a kiss. Instead, he flicked his tongue against the corners of my mouth, tasting the melon. Then, slowly and deliberately, he followed the trail down my chin, along my neck, to the spot where the juices had pooled in my collarbone.

He spent a lot of time there, cleaning off my skin. Licking. Sucking. One small, gentle, playful nip.

I think that's when my toes started to curl. He hadn't touched me with anything but his mouth and nowhere but my face and neck, and yet I was tingling all over.

"Mm, that was nice," he said.

"Nice," I echoed, my voice weak.

Okay, so I'd been wrong. Maybe this was about more than breakfast after all.

Please, let it be more than about breakfast.

I tried to talk, but the words caught. I cleared my throat, tried again. "I'm still hungry," I said, hoping the inflection implied something other than food. "How about you?"

"Ravenous." Cal peeled back the bedcovers and unbuttoned my bright yellow flannel nightshirt. He couldn't remove it, obviously, because my hands were tied, but it was enough for now. He tugged at my sleep shorts, white with smiley faces on them, and I raised my hips to help him out.

I spread my legs, a more-than-blatant hint.

Cal shook his head. "We've got all morning," he said. "Good...food should be savored."

With that, he selected a strawberry from the tray. Holding the green leaves between his fingers, he ran the berry along my chest, from collarbone to a spot just below my breasts. Every tiny, rough seed rasped individually against my skin.

My nipples were hard and dimpled, kind of like the fruit, by the time he got to them. He tickled the areolas, not quite giving me enough, not quite what I wanted. I moaned, wiggling my hips, giving him hints.

He laughed. He knew exactly what I wanted, but I was just going to have to wait for it.

"Open your mouth," he said.

I did, and he fed me the strawberry. I bit down, feeling my teeth crunch through the firm flesh, tasting the tart juice. I'd never known how sensuous eating could be.

I was drowning in the sensations when he slid the wet half of the strawberry right across my nipple.

My hips lifted right off the bed. The moisture on my breasts was nothing compared to the slickness growing between my legs.

Cal took his own sweet time suckling the juices off my nipple, nibbling and licking until I thought I would scream. I mean, was that really my breath, coming out in small gasps, sometimes punctuated by little whimpers?

He used fresh kiwi on my other breast, then kissed me again so I could taste what he'd been tasting.

If he didn't touch me soon...

I was hopeful when he brought forth the whipped cream, but he dipped a strawberry into it and circled both my nipples before feeding me the fruit. Only *then* did he clean me off.

And clean cream out of my belly button. I'm not sure how he managed to do that—my stomach was quivering from my need to come.

I was ready to come, and he hadn't even touched my clit yet. Hadn't so much as breathed on it.

Dammit, I wanted my hands free! As much as I was enjoying this, I wanted to run my fingers through his hair, bring his head up to mine for kisses.

Push his head down between my legs...

"Lick me," I begged, amazed at the way my voice trembled.

Cal grinned. "Already? We've barely gotten started."

I couldn't imagine he could be serious. But he was. I couldn't see the clock, but I was sure hours were going by as he fed me eggs Benedict with hollandaise sauce and salty ham, then managed to find all sorts of interesting spots like my hip bones to coat with sauce and then lick it away.

Sticky jam on the insides of my thighs. More whipped cream, in the hollows of my ankles. A heavenly taste of coffee, followed by him taking a mouthful and attacking my breasts again, so I felt the heat of the coffee mingled with his tongue and lips and teeth.

I wasn't even coherent by the time he dribbled champagne down my pussy.

I do know that the cold, fizzing bubbles started me over the edge seconds before Cal's mouth found my clit.

I do know I screamed, and the brass headboard slammed against the wall.

When I'd barely recovered from that, Cal slid his cock into me. My inner walls clenched around him, still pulsing from my orgasm. He lowered his head and kissed me. His mouth carried all the various tastes, salty and sweet, tart and savory, and the memory of all that he'd been doing to my helpless body made me convulse again. And again.

And more times than I could've counted, even if I'd been capable of thought.

After he untied me, we cuddled—that in itself was a rarity, and something I hadn't realized how much I missed. Not just the physical closeness, but the murmured conversation, the gentle laughter, the shared intimacy.

Eventually we wound around to the morning's events, and I asked him what had inspired him to such erotic creativity.

"Art at work—found out his wife was having an affair."

I really wasn't following this. I blamed the multiple, bed-shaking orgasms. "With you?"

Cal roared with laughter. "Not hardly! Her personal trainer."

"Oh." I tried to envision Art's wife. Pretty, with short dark hair and a fondness for pink toenail polish that matched her sandals.

"But it got me thinking," Cal said, sober now. "She'd told him things had gotten boring. She still loved him, but she'd gotten distracted by something different. I didn't want that to happen to us, Jennie."

Guiltily, I remembered my earlier thoughts of how we'd gotten into a rut. Much as I adored Cal with all my heart, I could understand the temptation to find the spark somewhere else.

Bless Cal for figuring out that we could reignite it.

I kissed him, slipped out of his embrace. We'd been lounging so long that the kids would be home soon.

"You made breakfast, so I'll clean up," I said.

He caught my wrist. "On one condition. When we have a few minutes, let's check the calendar and schedule another date."

My body tingled. I smiled. "Absolutely."

Before I was even out of the bedroom, I was already thinking about turning the tables on him. About drizzling honey on his hard cock. Honey's pretty sticky...it would take a long time to clean off...

And that would be just fine with me.

COUNTRY PLEASURES

Teresa Noelle Roberts

Ray gazed out the cottage window at the rain-drenched Galway village. "So much for the gorgeous light yesterday. It's all gray now. Not to mention pouring." He let out a melodramatic sigh, half self-mocking, half self-pitying.

"What do you expect? We're in Ireland," Jessica said. "Take wet, gray pictures today. Besides, it's not just gray. It's gray and green. Completely different from Santa Fe, and isn't that why you wanted to visit Ireland?"

He turned away from the window and nodded, although Jessica could tell he was still trying to cling to his grumpiness.

"You could take some great pictures—the castle ruins or the Neolithic tombs would look really romantic."

"You would think so. You and your passion for ruins." He smiled as he said it.

"Hey, without the passion for ruins, we might never have met." They'd bumped into each other while exploring an Anasazi site in the desert—Ray taking pictures, Jessica, a recent transplant from Ohio, soaking up the atmosphere. She'd been a history major in college, and while she'd never found a practical application for her studies, she enjoyed immersing herself in the past.

That, of course, was why she'd favored doing the Santa Fe/ Galway house swap—she could explore historical sites while Ray, an avid amateur photographer, took pictures in a new and different landscape. Hell, even the house was old by American standards, a genuine thatched cottage, restored by Dublin retirees blessed with both money and historic sensitivity. But now she wanted to be out of the cottage and seeing the sights.

Ray smiled. "I'm up for gray and misty shots—but not for underwater photography on land. How about we go back to bed until the rain lets up?" He nuzzled the back of her neck while his hands glided up to cup her T-shirt-clad breasts.

Jessica shivered pleasantly. Her nipples, still sensitive from their early-morning lovemaking, puckered at the touch. If Ray kept doing that, she'd soon be as wet inside as it was outside, and that would make exploring the countryside less inviting than exploring Ray once again. And the bed was a comfortable antique nest, topped with a feather bed....

Tempting. But Jessica looked out the window again. While they'd talked, the rain had slowed to a drizzle, and the sky was clearing. "Later!" she said, laughing. "How about we go up to the castle ruins?" She gestured in vaguely the right direction.

Ray peered out and hmmed. "I like the way the sun's breaking through the clouds."

"We can get lunch at the pub when we're done. Then we can come back and play indoors until it's time for sunset." She kissed him again.

Ray brightened at the mention of the pub. He might not be sold on Irish weather, but Irish beer was another story, and the seventeenth-century village pub promised photo opportunities in its own right. "I wonder how waterproof these boots are. Exploring won't be nearly as fun with wet feet."

"You New Mexico natives are such cats. But I think Claire and Martin left us something better for wet feet." Along with emergency numbers and directions to local sites, the homeowners had mentioned they'd left rainy-weather gear for their desert-dwelling visitors.

Jessica darted off to the closet.

Victory! Several pairs of tall rubber boots in different sizes were lined up in the closet and several rubber slickers hung on pegs. The closet smelled like rubber and damp. A note on the back of the closet door said, "Feel free to borrow Wellies and macs."

The boots in Jessica's size were bright red. An equally scarlet slicker with a hood, slightly too big and long enough on her small form that it hid her walking shorts, completed the ensemble. The boots and slicker closest to Ray's size were a more decorous shade of dark green.

She emerged feeling more than slightly ridiculous. "The ultimate sex symbol!" she joked, dropping Ray's boots and jacket to assume a cheesecake pose. Butt thrust out playfully, she peeked flirtily back over her shoulder. She had to bite her lip not to laugh.

And then she saw Ray's expression.

He was staring at her, or more to the point, at her boots and raincoat, like she *was* the ultimate sex symbol.

Very strange, but it was hard to resist the man she loved looking at her that way.

"You look adorable." He pressed up against her outthrust butt and nuzzled her shoulder. Or maybe he sniffed it, because his next words were, "And you smell good, too."

"I smell like a rubber raincoat."

"Is that what it is? I like it." He worked his hips against her, and even through the raincoat and his jeans she could feel his cock swelling.

At that, she couldn't help laughing, although it was a throaty, sexy laugh. "Perfume you don't notice, but this gets you all worked up?"

She could only see a little of his face with him pressed up behind her, but what she could see looked rapturous. "Yeah," he said, and he sounded rapturous too. "So sue me."

He pressed even closer and the raincoat crinkled. He seemed to enjoy that as well. "You have no idea how hot you look. You're so little and feminine, and the boots and coat are so big and clunky and practical looking. And shiny. And that smell mingling with your smell and the hints of sex from earlier...." He sniffed like a dog in the woods. "I can't get enough of it."

Okay, this was beyond weird. She knew some people were into rubber and latex, but she pictured such people wearing slinky rubber dresses or latex catsuits, not an outfit that made her feel like Paddington Bear.

On the other hand, while the outfit wasn't doing much for her, Ray's reaction to it was.

And if she played it right, she'd get to act on one of her favorite fantasies while indulging his. She'd always wanted to fool around in a castle. If she had to do it in Wellies and a slicker, so be it.

Heat surged through her at the thought.

He ran his hand below the raincoat, cupping her sex. "Damn, you're still wearing your shorts."

"For now. But they can come off later." She squirmed under his exploring fingers, wishing she was bare to his touch, but enjoying the diffused sensations spiraling through her sex. They filled her body with heavy warmth and her mind with evil ideas. "Like at that castle ruin."

His eyes widened. They'd talked about that fantasy a lot, but he'd always been nervous about the whole sex-in-public thing— even if it was a very private "public."

"Come on, I bet no one but a couple of crazy Americans will be up there on a day like this."

He looked her up and down and nodded slowly. "I guess it would be nearly as private as indoors—and a lot more romantic," he conceded, a nervous (or maybe excited) edge in his voice.

"Of course, you'll want to wear your Wellies and slicker too. Why don't you put them on while I go take care of a few things?"

Ray whipped her around, grinning like a man who'd been handed a dream. His eyes were full of love as he kissed her and caressed her body through the raincoat.

She broke away. "Be right back!" she exclaimed.

In the other room, she took off her clothes and shoved them into her day pack.

She shivered as the slicker went on over her bare skin. The cool, slightly sticky touch wasn't something she'd have thought of as erotic, but it turned her nipples into hard, eager points. Her belly was quivering from naughty nerves, and her vulva felt slick and swollen, pressing against itself as she moved.

Yeah, this was going to work, shades of Paddington Bear or no.

She returned to the main room to find Ray sporting a slicker, Wellies, and a beatific smile. His shorts and shirt were tossed on the floor. He was sniffing his own sleeve, looking like a cat indulging in catnip.

His slicker was tented in the front.

She grinned and grabbed his hand. "Let's go!"

They opted to drive as far as they could, leaving the walk for another, less sexually charged, time. The car park for the ruins was tiny, awash in mud, and other than their rental car, empty. The rain had stopped for the moment, leaving the ruined castle half obscured by mist and looking mysterious and inviting. She clenched at the thought that soon she and Ray would make love there.

Although warm, it was windier than Jessica had thought, and climbing the steep, rain-slicked trail in Wellies was awkward, but every time she started to think this had been a silly idea, Ray would kiss and caress her doubts away. She had to admit that his touch through the rubberized coat was different in an exciting way: cool and diffused, yet curiously intimate because of the look on Ray's face, the catch in his breath as he enjoyed the feel of her under the smooth, stiff material.

And Ray's reaction to her pressing his slicker against his swollen cock more than made up for cool, damp wind on her bare legs and the nagging suspicion that she looked ridiculous no matter how much Ray liked it. He squirmed against her, pleading inarticulately for more, and his cock felt huge and hard and hot through the rubber.

It took more willpower than she'd imagined to make it as far as the castle so they could fulfill both their fantasies at once.

The hollow windows, fallen walls, and stairs leading nowhere looked desolate and romantic in contrast with their damp, lushly green, wildflower-studded surroundings. Any other time, Jessica and Ray would have started poking around immediately, Ray taking pictures while Jessica attempted to reconstruct the castle in her mind and imagine the lives of the long-ago residents.

But the castle had been here since the fourteenth century; exploring it could wait a little longer.

Jessica's eyes were drawn to a tumbled wall that would be

just the right height for leaning over, but Ray had another idea. "I want pictures to remember this," he said, pulling his camera out of the mac's front pocket.

Of course. How many more chances would he have to get pictures of her naked in an Irish castle?

She started to unzip the slicker but he shook his head. "Oh, no, leave that on."

He took a whole series of pictures: Jessica posed in an archway, Jessica in her earlier cheesecake pose with her bare ass sticking out of the raincoat, Jessica above him on a wall so the focus was on the Wellies, Jessica lying on her back in the damp grass among the ruins, knees bent, so he could get a good shot of the muddy boots and her wet pussy, Jessica with the raincoat open to reveal her in all her naked, rubber-framed glory. She took a few of him too, although he wasn't too crazy about getting his picture taken, even with all his clothes on.

She started out laughing, but his intensity got to her and soon she was aflame with reflected desire, feeling as beautiful and sexy in her red Wellies as Ray thought she was.

And when he showed her the pictures, she could see it.

Now that she could see herself, she conceded flashing under a slicker was sexy in a playful '50s pinup way. And that shade of red looked good on her. But what really got to her were the pictures of Ray. He was usually so awkward in pictures, his good looks disguised by a pained, fake smile. In these, he was glowing, somewhere beyond aroused and on to ecstatic.

And that all the sexy pictures were taken in a castle in broad daylight didn't hurt one bit.

"I like the one," he said, "with you leaning over the wall, looking out over the hills. The way your pussy peeps out. I bet when we get it on the computer, it'll show how wet you are."

"I liked that one too," she said throatily. "I was thinking about you fucking me from behind."

His answer was simply, "God, yes!"

After the long teasing, she was more than ready and so was Ray. But she decided to give him one more treat. Sinking to her knees in the damp grass, she licked at his cock through the raincoat. She couldn't manage a full-out wrapped-in-rubber blow job because there wasn't enough play in the material, which was probably just as well; the flavor didn't do much for her. The slick, cool, mist-damp texture, with his heat emanating through, was another story. His moans, and his fingers tangling helplessly in her hair, went straight to her weeping pussy, making it contract around nothing and yearn to be filled. She wanted, oh, she wanted, but she took her time, teasing and pleasuring Ray until he grunted out, "Can't...take...much more."

Only then did she lead him to his chosen wall and bend over in blatant invitation. "Fuck me," she begged, and she didn't need to ask twice.

He eased inside her like friction had become obsolete.

For a few seconds they stayed fitted sweetly together, cock to pussy, skin to skin, rubber to rubber, enjoying the sensation and, in Jessica's case at least, the view of the Galway countryside with the village in the distance, the reminder that they were in a ruined Irish castle having sex.

Then Ray began to move, slowly at first, then faster and harder until he was stabbing deep inside her, hitting a spot that unfurled wave after wave of hot pleasure as red as her boots and coat. He clutched at her breasts through the raincoat, kneading just on the right side of almost too hard.

The stones bit into her hands and she kept bumping into the wall from the force of his thrusts, but the thought of souvenir bruises and scrapes from castle-sex added to her excitement.

Her orgasm built. Ray was lost in his own world, sniffing at her raincoat, muttering curses under his breath as he was trying to hold off coming.

Castle. Ray. Rubber. Ray. Kinky pictures. Ray, Ray, Ray.

Ray's cock pounding into her, Ray's hands caressing her, Ray's arousal, knowing she'd dared something new and liked it because Ray loved it...it was all too much.

Jessica clenched around the cock that filled her and cried out, startling a small flock of birds that she'd been too busy to notice until they flew off in a whir of wings and angry chirping.

"Love you," Ray gasped as he exploded inside her. "Love you...in Wellies."

They sank together to the grass, laughing and sighing.

And as they lay wrapped around each other and Ray talked about how they needed to buy Wellies of their own and replace these slickers with identical ones so they could claim the ones they'd fucked in, the sky opened and cool rain poured down.

"Well," Jessica laughed breathlessly, "it's a good thing we dressed for the weather."

FORBIDDEN FRUIT

Ric Amadeus

At noon, she entered his study with a plate of food. He had been up since five, disturbing her only slightly as he climbed out of bed. She had spent the morning picking fruits from their organic garden, while he worked tirelessly to complete his research paper.

"Lunch, darling?"

"I'm too busy," he said, fervently working his scientific calculator as he scribbled and erased, scribbled and erased on a tattered sheet of quadrille graph paper. A half-dozen books were spread across his desk: *Pesticide Residue in California Watersheds, Malathion Studies Annual, Ethnobotany Digest 1984, Problems in Biochemistry, Agricultural Pest Control and Cancer, Bug Spray and You.* His computer flashed long strings of numbers, the pop-up window showing a blue bar slowly creeping past 24 percent as it worked on calculations needed to prove his thesis.

She set the tray down on top of his papers and leaned

against the edge of his desk, well aware that her pink bikini
top, a fetching and saucy garment with cherries adorning the
pink fabric, didn't hide much of the fetching swell of her breasts.
Her tight jean shorts were unbuttoned at the top, revealing
the matching cherry-print bottoms underneath and the candy
red tattoo of an apple just above the waistline of the low-cut
bottoms that featured the scripted legend: ORGANICALLY GROWN
Her long, smooth legs were dusted with the soil of the garden,
and her smooth belly swelled slightly from all the organic
morsels she'd eaten as she picked. The tiny bulge accented
the sparkling silver ring through her navel and the tattoo.
Her full, kissable lips were still stained red with the juice of
organic cherries.

She said, "Baby, you've got to eat."

He looked up at her angrily, pushed his chair back, and
sighed.

"But I'm close to solving this problem," he said. "I'm close
to establishing beyond the shadow of the doubt that pesticide
consumption is responsible for the destructive and uncontrol-
lable rise in chronic hypersexuality in adolescent females."

"Adults, too?" she asked nervously.

"That remains to be seen," he said, his eyes narrowed and his
lips pursed. "Further study is needed."

"But you should eat," she said. "You didn't even have breakfast."

"I had a cup of coffee," he said defensively. "The organic
decaf Guatemalan."

"We're out of soy milk," she said.

"I drank it black," he told her.

"If you lose your strength, you'll never prove your thesis."
She bent down low and kissed him on the cheek, her barely clad
breasts gently brushing his arm. "Take a break, have some food,

and you'll feel so much better. Everything will become clear after lunch."

He sighed, took off his glasses, rubbed his eyes. "All right," he said. "I'll have some lunch."

"Come sit on the couch with me," she said. "It's good to get away from your desk." She picked up the tray and carried it over to the small, tattered sofa that adorned his study. She set the tray on the coffee table while he joined her, looking grumpy and angry that she was making him eat. This sort of thing happened frequently, though; he was such a dedicated scientist that he very often forgot to nourish himself—ironic beyond measure for a man whose lifework lay in proving the dangers of pesticide use and the advantages of organic farming.

She knew that once he ate, everything would seem different.

She poured him a glass of thrice-filtered water and took the unbleached cotton napkin off of the beautiful assortment of sliced apples, cherries, oranges, unyeasted home-baked bread, and yogurt-cultured soy cheese that she had prepared for him.

"I guess I am pretty hungry," he said, and seized a piece of bread. He ate quickly, piling three slices of soy cheese on three slices of bread and adding a small slice of apple to each.

"The one thing I can't figure out," he said, holding a fragrant morsel near his lips, "is what kind of effect this pesticide-induced hypersexuality would have on a man. The data is clear for young women—with improper pesticide use, they become completely unable to control themselves."

"Explains a lot," she said, leaning back into the softness of the sofa and propping her shapely legs on the coffee table. "You know, I'm younger than you."

He waved his hand dismissively. "But you've been raised on organic produce. Thank god for your parents, particularly your father. If it hadn't been for his critical early work in nourishing you entirely on organics, I might never have been able to carry the torch. Now, I'm close to a breakthrough."

Her eyes lowered and she flushed slightly. She looked at the food poised so teasingly near his mouth.

"Eat your apple, darling," she said.

He stuffed his mouth full of food and washed it down with filtered water, barely taking time to chew. As he swallowed, his eyes narrowed.

"Is that your new swimsuit you're wearing?" he asked.

She smiled shyly, running her hands down over the full swells of her ample breasts. The nipples had begun to peek through the pale fabric.

"Yes it is," she said. "But I don't think I could get much swimming done while wearing it."

"That's for sure," he said.

"Do you like it?"

His eyes widened and he drank in the beauty of her tits while he chewed another slice of apple. "I love it," he said. "Fuck, it's amazing. Your tits...your tits are incredible."

She smiled. "You never call them that."

"I guess I don't," he said, his mouth stuffed so full she could barely understand his words. "God, they're magnificent. Why have I never noticed how magnificent they are?"

"I remember you thinking they were magnificent last night," she said, smiling.

"Did we make love last night?" he mused, reaching for another apple slice. "I can't recall. My mind must have been engaged."

She frowned bitterly.

"Have another slice of apple, dear. They're good for you."

As he chewed, his eyes grew wider and he seemed unable to take them off of her tits. She could see his cock swelling in his polyester pants, stretching them noticeably. She looked at him and licked her lips.

"Would you like to see them bare?" she asked.

"I need to get back to work," he said, his voice hoarse. "As soon as I'm finished eating...."

"No harm in looking while you eat, is there?" she asked, and pulled the front of her bikini top down.

His eyes, now as wide as they could get, drank in the lush beauty of her full tits with their pink nipples. He absently placed another apple slice in his mouth and chewed as she ran her fingers over her breasts, pinching her nipples gently.

"Nice, aren't they?"

"Beautiful," he uttered in a barely comprehensible mumble around half-chewed pieces of fruit. His hand had found its way into his crotch.

"Do you realize you're stroking your crotch, darling?" she asked.

He swallowed. "Am I?" he muttered absently, rubbing his cock more firmly through his pants. "God, I can't take my eyes off of you."

"You don't need to," she said. "Keep eating." She reached out and handed him another three slices of apple, then unfastened her bikini top and slipped it off. She tossed it away so that it draped over the plate of food. She began to caress her own tits.

"You want to touch them, don't you?" she asked. "They're like ripe fruit to you. Ripe...organic...fruit."

"I can't," he said, stroking his cock with one hand while he stuffed food into his mouth with the other. "I need to work."

"What's the harm in a little touch?" she said. "But wait, there's more of me to touch." She pulled down her shorts and wriggled out of them, planting one foot up on the back of the sofa so that her calf brushed his shoulder. The cherry-print bikini bottoms were so skimpy that he could see the swollen lips of her pussy around the crotch, poking out from where they'd been tugged free as she bent over in the garden.

"Oh, my god," he burbled through apple and soy cheese. "That's so magnificent." His fingers tightened around the swell of his cock, and as she lifted her legs high in the air and peeled off the bikini bottoms, he moaned softly through fruit pulp and began to stroke faster.

"Fuck," he moaned as she spread her legs wide, lifting her hips so he could better see her ripe, open pussy with its glistening sheen of sexual juice. "That's incredible."

She reached out, wriggled her fingers under the bikini top that now partially hid the plate of food, and produced an apple slice. She slid it slowly up the inside of her thighs and tucked it between her pussy lips.

"Keep eating," she told him breathlessly. "You need food."

He lunged forward desperately, knocking over his thrice-filtered water and spraying it across the floor. His mouth molded to her cunt and he sucked down the apple hungrily, but her thighs closed around his face and she held his hair firmly, grinding her sex against his seeking mouth as he began to tongue her eagerly. She writhed on the sofa as his mouth worked her clit, and he no longer seemed interested in protesting that he had work to do. On the contrary, when finally she arched her back and moaned in orgasm, she had to pull his head away from her sex because she just couldn't take any more.

She undulated beneath him, her naked skin flushed, her lips still red with cherry. She looked up into his eyes, her hunger obvious.

"Fuck me," she moaned.

As he leapt on her and fervently clawed at the fly of his polyester pants, she plucked an apple and put it in her mouth. She then seized his hair and pulled his mouth to hers, pushing the apple onto his tongue as they kissed. His cock came free and he entered her smoothly, finding her pussy wetter than his absent mind had ever noticed it to be. He moaned as he plunged into her and started fucking her with unprecedented ardor, his hands molding to her tits as her tongue savaged his mouth between chewing motions. She cupped his cheeks with her hands and pulled his cock deeper into her, lifting her hips to meet each powerful thrust. When she came again, she snuggled close to him and begged him to take her upstairs before he finished with her.

With his eyes glazed, he pulled out of her and felt her mouth on his slick cock as she licked him clean, eagerly letting her tongue caress his balls, his shaft, and his swollen head. When he bleated softly, once, "Work..." she reached out and grabbed another slice of apple, stuffing it in his mouth to silence him.

When he was right on the edge of coming in her mouth, her lips left his cock and she looked up at him.

"Take me to bed," she begged.

He chased her up the stairs, shedding his clothes as he went. When she climbed abed on hands and knees and put her ass in the air, legs spread, pussy exposed and still moist from his spit and the juice coaxed forth by his hard fucking, he didn't even think to pause. He joined her on the bed and drove into her with a hunger that made her whimper in rapturous pleasure. He reached under her to hold her magnificent tits as he ravished her from behind, fucking her so hard that she came twice more as she rubbed her clit, then begged for his come inside her. He let himself go deep in her pussy and collapsed on top of her.

Within moments he was snoring, and over the next six hours he woke up only twice, when she could resist temptation no more

and he found her sliding her mouth onto his cock and her pussy
onto his hungry mouth. Each time he satisfied her, fucking her in
as many positions as either of them could come up with before
finally coming inside her. His life's work was forgotten, a tangle
of scattered and meaningless papers much, much less important
than his insatiable hungers and her delicious, naked body.

When finally he awakened on his own, late in the evening, he did
so with a gasp and a long, low moan of horror.

"What's the matter, darling?" she asked in a whisper, her face
tucked against his bare chest.

"What have you done?" he sighed. "Oh, darling, what have
you done?"

She cleared her throat and said nonchalantly, "Why, whatever do you mean, baby?"

"That apple," he said. "It was from the control group."

She reddened, clutched him close.

"I'm sorry, baby. You were so caught up in your work. I...I
couldn't take it anymore. I needed a little attention."

"Oh, what have you done?"

She sat up and put one finger across her lover's lips. "Shh,
baby," she cooed. "At least we've proved your premise. And it
works on men, too."

She cradled him in her hand, gently stroking his shaft. It
quickly began to grow hard, and she kissed her way down his
chest as he moaned softly with pleasure. When her mouth found
his cock, his hands came to rest gently in her long, dark hair,
stroking her as her head bobbed up and down on him.

"Oh, what have you done," he moaned, but this time he
sounded less convinced. "Eve, Eve, what have you done?"

There was a distant hissing from the organic garden.

NOONER

Bella Dean

Jack's car is there when I get home from work. The shades are drawn, the door is shut, but his car fills the drive. I'm so tired my eyes are burning. My feet hurt, and all I want is an omelet and soda and to fall buck naked into my bed. My shift was hellacious, my drive stressful. All the way home from the hospital my CHECK ENGINE light glowed at me, an evil red scary eye.

I unlock the door, annoyed to have to do so. Didn't he hear my car? Can't he unlock the door? Or maybe he's sick. Maybe he's asleep. All of this swirls through my muddled mind. I fling open the door half exhausted, half annoyed. Not in the best mood it seems.

"What are you doing here? Are you sick?" I demand.

"Hello, to you, too, Jen," Jack says and then grins. He runs his hands through his dark blond hair and rubs his eyes. He smiles again, happy to see me, and it diffuses my anger just a touch.

"Sorry, babe. Hi. Now, what are you doing here? Are you

sick?" I drop my bag by the door and try not to yawn. I need a nice "dinner" and then sleep. Glorious, glorious sleep. My body is still resisting my new vampire status. Work from three to eleven, home, food, bed. I feel like I hardly ever see my husband anymore and here I am being snippy with him.

He puts his hands out to me and I go to him, kicking off my heels as I go. The carpet kisses my stocking feet and I groan aloud. It just feels so fucking good to be free of those shoes. I sink onto his lap and he kisses my throat. "Mmm. So it's a secret then?"

"No. Just wanted to kiss you first. You look all hot and professional." His hand tickles up my thigh and I smack it away.

"Answer me!"

"Oh, right. Sorry. I got distracted by your stockings. I am taking advantage." Jack's hand creeps higher and I smack it again but laugh. "Oh, sorry. I am taking advantage of the company's work-from–home-to-save-gas-and-sanity clause. I am getting twice as much work done in half the time because no one is asking me dumb-ass questions or making me sing 'Happy Birthday' or asking me to spot the receptionist's desk because she's gone into false labor. Again." His hand rubs warm circles on my leg and my hose whisper secretly. I shift in his lap and realize his cock is hard.

"Except your wife. I'm still asking dumb-ass questions." I wiggle some more and I'm not so hungry anymore. I'm more interested in my man and his cock than a cheese omelet and seven hours of sleep.

"Your questions are not dumb-ass at all but your ass is quite fine. And wife? I don't have a wife. " Jack's hand has slipped up under the hem of my very sensible black skirt. His calluses rasp against my thigh-highs and his fingers tickle at the edge of my panties. I feel a trickle of warmth between my legs from his touch. My panties are now wet and my body is warm and ready. Like magic, he has turned me on.

"No? My mistake, I thought you were married." I lean in and kiss him where his stubble is the thickest. My tongue traces his red lower lip and he grabs the back of my head and kisses me hard. His mouth is hot and sweetly familiar but the game is enough to add a nasty secret thrill to the kiss.

"I'm so glad you came when you did, I really need an assistant for some dictation."

It's eleven thirty in the morning and I should be eating and winding down for bed. Instead, I'm playing dirty make-believe with my Jack. It's worth the lost sleep. I smile and try not to laugh out loud. I try to stay in character. In my best sultry siren voice I say, "I have a reputation for being extremely good at taking *dic*-tation." I wiggle my ass over his erection and he makes a desperate sound deep in his throat.

"Really? I give big dictation. Can you handle my big dictation?"

We both giggle but keep up with the charade. I cover a snort. Bite my lip. Smile at him and he smiles back. But then his fingers pinch my nipple through my silk blouse, through my bra. The harsh bite of pain is white hot. I suck in a breath and shiver with surprise. Jack reaches down and pops my little shiny black buttons one by one. The blouse falls open and we both look at my black lace bra as if it is a work of art. Which it kind of is, it's so pretty and delicate. He thumbs my nipples and they stand up for him, sweetly flushed beneath the lace.

"I think I can handle whatever you have to give me, sir." My heart is skipping around in my chest and I feel like I can't get a deep breath. Why am I getting so excited by our little game? Don't know. Don't care. I wiggle my ass some more. I have gone past flirty to whorish and I love it.

"You are such a slut," Jack says, reading my mind. "And sluts are only good for one thing," he growls. He pushes my shoulders none too gently and I lower myself between his legs. He thrusts up and I pry open his jeans like I'm opening a present.

I free him from his boxers and stare at his lovely hard cock—lovely and hard for me. The me who is not his wife. The me who's a tramp for him. The assistant that came to his rescue at just the right moment in time. "I'm only a slut for you, sir," I confess and lick my lips before parting them.

I have spent eight hours distributing and overseeing medical records and I'm exhausted. But here I am thrilled to be on my knees in my very own dining room, kneeling before my husband and making him shift and groan and pant because my very wet lips are a fraction of an inch from his cock. I lower my head so that my breath flows over him and his hard flesh twitches from my close proximity. I lower myself another hair's breadth but do not touch. Do not suck. Do not lick. I wait. Let him suffer. Let him beg. Let him—

"Suck it, bitch," he says, and pushes my shoulders down. The cruelty in his tone and the bite of his words make my pussy go wet and ready for him. He never talks to me that way and here he is ordering me, holding me still, fucking up into my mouth hard enough to make me gasp.

My eyes water and I squirm. I would give anything to be free of my panties. Free of my clothes. They seem to weigh a thousand pounds, bonds of cotton and silk and lace. I try to keep up with him, take him deep into my throat. He stops pushing my shoulders but not his thrusting. His trim hips bang an excited tattoo on the wooden seat. "God, Jen. Jesus."

"Sir?" I manage before he's filling my throat again and fisting my hair in his hands. He yanks hard enough to make me sob and growls low in his throat.

"Enough. Enough. Come up here."

The game has shifted from giggles to orders. From joking to intense. His brown eyes are heavy, his face flushed, his dick nearly purple. The grandfather clock ticks on monotonously in the corner. Dusty shafts of sunlight decorate my carpet. I stand.

"Dictation," he says. His grin awakens a low-level buzzing fear in my belly but my cunt twitches with anticipation. I want him. I want him to be rough with me and call me names and make me cry. And yes, hurt me just enough to make me come hard.

We've only been here a few times but when we visit it is good. The Jack who makes me cry a little makes me come a lot.

He pushes a pad and a pen in front of me. He bends me forward at the waist so my body is sprawled on the table and my ass is high, his own personal X-rated Barbie doll: *bend her, pose her, punish her, fuck her.* I giggle and then bite my tongue.

"What's funny, girl?" Something cool and smooth runs over my ass. The ass he has suddenly bared by shoving up my skirt and pulling down my bikini panties. It feels like plastic and he traces my asscheeks with it, runs a nearly sharp edge down the crack of my ass. I jump a little.

"Nothing."

Crack! It's a ruler and it has a blistering kiss when he wields it. My breath catches and I whimper.

"What? What did you say?"

"Nothing, *sir*," I amend.

"The light signal at Avon and Simms is off by seven seconds." He runs the now-threatening plastic over my hot skin. A throb has started on my left asscheek.

"What?"

Two more cracks and my hips bang the edge of the dining room table. The table I will serve Thanksgiving dinner on.

Corporal punishment, anyone? I giggle, sob. All my wires are crossed.

"Dictation, Jennifer," he reminds me and gives me a stroke on each cheek so I remember.

I start to write and he shoves a finger into my pussy. Presses the bundles of nerves that make my cunt tighten and then release. I'm a kiss away from coming and he knows it.

Had he said Axis and Savoy? Ten seconds? Five? Was it a light or a signal? My hands are shaking and my cunt is pulsing and my brain seems to be quite preoccupied with him shoving his cock as deep into me as he can get and fucking me until I can't remember what a cheese omelet is, let alone that I wanted one earlier.

"Read that back," he says and pushes another thick finger into my pussy.

My vision doubles...trebles...from unshed tears, and a hysterical laugh burbles out of me. *Whack, whack, whack!* screams the ruler.

"The signal at Axiam and Sinclair is off by six seconds," I say, praying that even some of that is right.

The room is suddenly charged. Jack is not moving. Shit, I can barely hear him breathing. His hand has withdrawn from me and my ass is stinging like it's on fire. I can't quite tell where he is behind me, and I am now afraid because I am pretty sure that none of that was right.

None.

The hairs on my arms stand up and I feel the sharp edge of the ruler trace each line of my buttocks. It slides like a dull razor up my ass crack again. Jack presses it flat against my clit. It's a cool impersonal kiss on my swollen skin. He moves it in gentle circles until pleasure uncurls in me and then his voice, menacing and dark says, "That wasn't even close."

Six whacks in a row. Six sharp plastic smacks against my clit and I am crying. But then he is making that animal sound that comes from somewhere in his chest and the velvet steel head of his cock is penetrating me.

He goes slow and I can tell it is maddening to him to make himself be patient. But he's punishing me some more. He's making me wait and behave and most definitely not push back to impale myself. This Jack is all about discipline.

"Say it after me." He's halfway in, Mr. Traffic Engineer who's going to teach me how to pay attention. "The light signal..."

"The light signal," I gasp. His fingers are digging into my skin and I can tell he is marking me on purpose. Purple echoes of his fingertips will be on my body for days.

"At Avon and Simms," he growls. He's thrusting harder and I feel his finger brush my lips and I lick it, lick it again. Then he's pushing it into my ass, swift and intense. The bite of pain has me pressing my forehead to the green tablecloth and panting.

"At Avon and Simms," I bark. I'm gripping the table and trying not to thrust back. He'll stop if I do. Instead I concentrate on holding off my orgasm and pushing my belly flush to the table as he fucks me and his finger fucks my ass.

"Is off—"

"Is off—" I mimic, a naked slutty parrot.

"By seven seconds."

"By seven seconds. Oh, god, please Jack. Let me—" He slams into me hard and that nudges me right over the edge.

Then Jack is coming with me and somewhere in there we are laughing again.

He lies flush to my back, cock still inside of me. His denim shirt tickles my chin, his stubble rakes me. "You sure suck at dictation but you are a damn good lay, baby."

"Thank you, sir."

I yawn and the grandfather clock gives us twelve celebratory bongs. "Bedtime for me soon. Want to join me?"

"I can't. I've got work to do. But I'll make you something to eat and bring it to you when you get out of the shower." He kisses the back of my neck and I shiver under him. He's back to himself now.

"Deal."

I pass him, my shirt hanging open, my skirt still bunched around my waist. He smacks my already hot ass and I yelp.

"But thanks for the nooner, toots," he says.

"Any time, sir. Any time."

ANOTHER HOLE WEEK

Jeremy Edwards

Monday

Today is Monday, and Lucille's tickle hole is near the heel of her right stocking. That is, it's on the sole; but it's way back at the rear end of things, so it doesn't give me access to the really tender meat at the heart of the foot—where I know from experience that half a tickle would be enough to moisten Lucille's panties.

No, I'm going to have to work at this today. And now that her shoes are on, I may not get a crack at her tickle hole du jour until the *jour* is almost over. I think she'll be out with clients most of the morning, anyway (hence the stockings).

I'm in luck, though, because after lunch she decides to chill on the couch with the arts section for fifteen minutes. And the shoes, naturally, come off. I'm slightly allergic to the smell of newspaper ink, but I'll put up with that for a chance to insinuate a finger into the tight yawn of a stocking hole.

When I make myself comfortable on the sofa cushion next to Lucille, her foot finds its way to my lap, as if by instinct. My finger penetrates, but at first she doesn't notice—or else she's teasing me by pretending she doesn't. So I patiently trace circles on the toughened flesh, half-imagining that I'm touching her clit or her asshole.

She puts the paper down and closes her eyes, and I know that she's now focused on me. (Lucille is not an afternoon napper.) As my circles get more defined—then more irregular—then lighter—then more passionate, her foot squirms in my hand. For seven glorious seconds, she giggles to my touch. Then she pulls her foot away, kisses me on the forehead, and returns to her desk. She leaves me the paper, and the scent of her aroused cunt—which easily supersedes that of the irritating ink.

Tuesday

A lazy golfer would love today's tickle hole. It floats directly over Lucille's winking navel—a shot no one could miss. Call me a lazy bastard ("golfer" doesn't apply to me), but I'd like to spend hours here.

This plum-colored top is one of my favorite items in her wardrobe. And the tired cotton, thus far, has given up in only the one place. As we put away the breakfast paraphernalia, the hem of the untucked jersey glides this way and that, giving the illusion that a summer breeze has shown a miraculous disregard for the closed kitchen windows. And so while Lucille is in motion, the tickle hole lines up with her belly button only at certain moments. I mentally keep score, logging each time they match up as a point in some undefined bank.

I have to go out, and she embraces me good-bye. While we kiss, I find the tickle hole without looking—I know where Lucille's navel is, after all—and her belly swirls sensuously for me as I tickle it in super slo-mo.

We're still kissing. She doesn't want to let go, doesn't want the low-simmer tickling to stop. Her knees bump against mine as she squeezes her thighs together. "Fuck me tonight," she says when our lips part. She grabs my wrist and works my hand like a sex toy, tickling herself with it. Her horny laughter rings in my ears all day.

Wednesday
Today, Lucille's tickle hole is hidden so well that it takes me half the day to find it. *Holy fuck,* I say to myself, duly impressed when I've finally located it. *It's inside the left asscheek pocket of her Levi's.* It's a good thing I felt the impulse to goose her, or who knows how long I'd have been stumped. (And suppose I'd been right-handed?) The goose doesn't count as a tickle. Lucille and I are certain to agree on this, so no discussion of the matter is even necessary.

We also don't need to discuss the practicality of my pressing my erection-hard jeans into her rear seam. I do this while I caress the secret denim inside her pocket and tease the tickle hole into letting my pinkie in; cock to crack is clearly the logical position for me to assume in undertaking the delicate maneuvers required for tickling Lucille on this busy Wednesday.

She wears no panties beneath her snug Levi's today, so it's raw ass flesh at my fingertip. She wriggles into me while I titillate the only square centimeter of her derriere that my finger can reach. Judging from the warm, urgent softness of her denim cheeks against my denim cock, teasing that one centimeter is as good as a full-bottom erotic massage right now. I tickle her till I think I'm going to come—meaning not very long—and send her on her way with a left-handed "love your ass" slap. My IOU.

As she scoots off toward a ringing phone, I feel pretty sure that she's copied the aforementioned promissory note onto the crotch of her jeans, in molten girlcome.

Thursday

Why should I go to the trouble of tickling Lucille through the sweatband on her wrist, when the rest of her beautiful arm is entirely naked? Because I can't resist a tickle hole, that's why—and she knows it.

Oh, don't worry: I also kiss up and down that sun-gold tennis skin; lick the shower-fresh underarm; and gently sample the parabola of her shoulder with my teeth. But it's all to the tempo of that *tickle-tickle-tickle* on her wrist, where I stroke her like a whispering second hand.

This tickle hole frames her pulse, and the pulse, quickening, strokes me back. Can a finger have an orgasm? Mine could be the first.

Her arm swings with me, hedonistically, like a hammock that's anchored to my pointer. Her cheeks flush, and she giggles languidly, in spurts, in a manner reminiscent of bubbles slowly birthing over ice cubes in a frosted glass. My mind is soon filled with a giant image of moist tennis panties.

Lucille never misses her game, and I know today will be no exception. I wish I could lie on the clay, squint up in the sunlight, and watch her juice baking dry under her skirt.

Tickle-tickle-tickle. Tickle-tickle-TOCK.

She's saturated, for now. Satiated will come later.

In the midst of scrambling to gather her things, she tosses me an independent, pristine pair of white knickers from her dresser. She doesn't have time to explain that she expects to find my come stains on them when she returns in two hours. I figure it out, though.

Friday

It's cooler today, and this explains Lucille's turtleneck—the one with the tickle hole, right at the seam where the neck piece meets the collar line. Around back.

The neck of her shirt has some type of synthetic blended into it, which means there's more latitude here than would be afforded by a similarly situated cotton tickle hole. Without stressing the material, I'm able to push my erect finger up at just about any angle I want, and Lucille's nape becomes my playground.

Her curls, girly on my knuckles, tickle the tickler as she moves her head. I'm not sure who's being seduced and who's doing the seducing, but that's part of the beauty of it. Tickling Lucille's neck makes some of the muscles tense up while others relax. She says it's analogous to how her cunt feels when we build her toward an orgasm: clenched here, undone there, tight, loose, flowing, coiled in anticipation like when a roller coaster crests...and (she says) "Oh, fucking wow, you're making me come." And she's actually going to have an orgasm, maybe not even a minor one, because I'm tickling the tingly smoothness of her neck. It helps that she's not wearing a bra, so that my other hand can pinch her left nipple through the clingy material of her shirt. And it helps that her own hand is in her pants, managing her clit, channeling my tickles.

Soon she doesn't even need the tickles. She recedes from my touch—honey giggling off the edge of a piece of toast—and crouches onto herself, rubbing and rubbing.

Saturday

As soon as I wake up, I observe that there's a small hole in Lucille's baby blue panties, where the gusset coats her lips: a miniature cunt, poised above the real thing.

She doesn't yet realize that I'm awake, and I study her quietly. While I watch, her hand finds the hole, and she utilizes it as a gateway into herself. Her finger is so elegant, silently poking into her own desire-plumped flesh. I don't know whether to get involved or just keep watching.

The decision is made for me. The bed creaks when I grab my industrial-strength morning erection, and Lucille's eyes meet mine. Initially, her finger doesn't stop what it's doing. Then she removes it—not without a hint of reluctance on her face—and she offers it to me to taste. It's an especially potent treat, first thing in the morning.

After this overture, she rests her head on folded arms, which in turn rest on her pillow. The wiggle of her bottom would serve as an invitation, were any further invitation needed.

She's so slick that I'm tempted to serve her a solid finger-fucking à la carte, without any preliminaries. But no. It's a tickle hole. So I dally just inside the rent fabric, making her ass churn and her pussy juice flow. She laughs that perfect laugh that means it's almost too tickly but not quite—in other words, she's getting maximum pleasure, every ounce she can take without having to pull away. I keep it up, taking care not to overdo it but making sure I don't slack off. Meanwhile, I yank on the top elastic of the panties and bring my face to her cheeks, nuzzling and licking.

And now she's going to come like hell. She's grinding her pelvis on the firm mattress to get her clit going, and I stick my finger all the way into her and give her ass slap after tender slap inside the panties. The tickle giggles morph into orgasm giggles—and if you don't know the difference, you've never tickled and fucked Lucille. The orgasmic giggles are bigger and rounder. They're also denser, like seeds; I swear that you could plant them in the carpet and grow new orgasms from them.

I leave my finger in the tickle hole and the Lucille hole while she clutches my cock. I tickle, she giggles; her fingers vibrate, I giggle too. Sweet fuck, I don't last ten seconds.

Sunday

It's Sunday morning. When I return from the gym, I find Lucille sprawling on the couch, in the nude.

"Mmm…" I say by way of a greeting. I squeeze onto the couch, and her breasts press into me as I kiss her. "But where's the tickle hole?"

"Silly man," she says. "Where *isn't* the tickle hole?"

She's right. Lucille is all tickle hole today. One big tickle hole that leaves no room for clothing—or, if you prefer, an infinite number of contiguous tickle holes, with no fabric separating them.

And this, of course, means that she can be tickled anywhere. Where to begin? Decisions, decisions. Lucille is better at making them than I am, and she takes the initiative, leading my hand to her nipple. I tickle around it, and her hips gyrate.

She moves my hand to the vicinity of her knee. I reach under it, to where the sensitive indentation works with the sofa to form a little cave. Into the cave goes my hand, and it doesn't take much to get Lucille giggling.

She wants me all over the crack of her ass next. So, needless to say, that's exactly where I am. Her bottom dances and dances while I pretend my hand is a feather.

Now I make a decision. I separate Lucille's vanilla thighs, and I tickle her pussy lips.

"*Yesssss,*" she manages between giggles, bouncing herself away from, then back onto, my pleasuring finger. She greedily takes as much of the stimulation as she can, then gives herself a brief rest…then returns for more. This goes on for two or three pussy-dripping minutes, until she's had her fill.

My cock is thick and hard and aching, and I can't remember anything as satisfying as this sensation of sliding into her wet, tickle-primed, tickle lover's love hole.

I'd thought Lucille was all tickled out for the moment, but

she seems to have found a second wind. She guides my left hand under her right arm. "Don't stop till I ask you to," is the request kissed into my ear, and I begin to integrate a gentle delighting of her underarm into the rhythm of my hungry fuck-thrusts. I keep expecting her to ask me to stop; but she's evidently reached some sort of sweet plateau, where it's perfectly intense without being too much, and all she says is my name, over and over.

She's coming, and still she wants me to tickle her, to take her through every instant of her orgasm. I'm blinded by the heat of my own climax when she finally comes down, says, "Okay," with a last giggle, and moves my hand away. She kisses my face repeatedly while I pump and groan.

Afterward, in her hot bath, she tells me she's still so aroused that every cell of her skin seems erogenous. I touch her somewhere on the triceps region of her arm, and she moans as if I'm tonguing her between the legs.

Lucille sinks slowly into the bubbles until they clothe her fully from the neck down. Then I see a gap developing in the suds on her upper chest, slightly below her collarbone. I look at this oasis of epidermis within the weave of froth, and I smile. Even the bubbles know that my Lucille always has to have a tickle hole.

CHLOE'S CONFESSION

Sophia Valenti

When I began dating Chloe, I'd noticed that her eyes sometimes strayed when a good-looking guy passed us by. But she was even more likely to ogle a hot girl—and nudge me with her elbow to make sure I didn't miss her. It never bugged me. In fact, I thought it was kind of cool that she'd forget what she was talking about as she stared longingly at a woman's fine rear end. Somewhere, deep down, I guess I was hoping I'd get to live the typical man's fantasy: to watch your girl get it on with another gorgeous lady, and then get invited to join in the fun. But much like everything else in my life with Chloe, what actually happened was far from typical.

I'd dated quite a few girls in my day, but rarely did my attention stay focused for long. Which leads me to the first thing that surprised me about Chloe—the fact that I couldn't get her out of my head. Two days after a Friday night dinner date, I was still fantasizing about the way she tasted, and I felt the ghost of her lips wrapped around my cock. Needing to see her again

before I headed into a seemingly endless workweek, I decided
to pay her a surprise visit. Undaunted by the gloom of a dreary
Sunday afternoon, I made my way through a midday rainstorm,
jumping over puddles and dodging taxis as I headed across town
to her place.

When she answered the door—sans makeup and wearing her
shoulder-length auburn hair in adorable pigtails—she brightened my day in a way sunshine never could. Her beauty helped
dispel the dampness and made me forget everything but her
smile. She welcomed me warmly and ushered me inside, but
as I crossed the threshold, I nearly gasped. It looked like her
closet had exploded—there were clothes everywhere. When she
announced she was spring-cleaning, I actually laughed out loud.
Dirty dishes were in the sink, the ceramic kitchen floor tiles
desperately needed mopping, and her rain-spattered windows
were coated with grime.

"Seriously—you're cleaning?" I asked incredulously.

"Well, sort of," she said, smiling sheepishly. "You know: new
season, new boyfriend—" She looked at me coquettishly from
under her long lashes, and when I smiled, she continued, "New
panties."

That's when I took a closer look at the riot of color nearly
overwhelming her tiny studio apartment. The floor was literally
paved with panties. There were so many pairs scattered about,
I could walk across the room and never actually have my feet
touch her hardwood floor. There were cotton boy-shorts, lacy
thongs, satin briefs—far too many to count. I bent down and
picked up a pair of ruby red silk string bikinis from a nearby
pile. As I toyed with the slick material, it felt like water slipping through my fingers. My cock twitched in recognition as I
lost myself in the mental image of the garment stretched tightly
across her sleek, shaved mound. In my mind I could see the bold

silk hugging her curves, the cotton-paneled crotch slightly darker
from the juice seeping from her aroused sex. My mouth watered
at the thought of tonguing her slit through those flimsy undies.

"But why would you get rid of these?" I asked, when I'd finally
recovered my ability to speak. "They're practically new."

Chloe blushed prettily as she confessed, "Oh, I used to wear
them for James. Actually, I wore a lot of these for him. He bought
them for me." She glanced around at the panties surrounding her
feet. And while I sensed she was somewhat abashed, I could also
see that her memories excited her. Her apple-sized breasts rose
and fell in time with her deep breaths, which were becoming
slightly more erratic, and she bit her lip the way she does when
I tease her thighs with whisper-soft kisses. "Those are his favorites," she added with a sigh, nodding toward the pair in my
hands.

My stomach began to churn as I pictured some other guy
peeling this silken wrapper off Chloe's shapely figure. I balled
up the panties in my fist as I struggled to get hold of my temper.
"Who's James?" I asked haltingly.

"He's an ex, but we're still friends. It was nothing serious. It
was just a fling."

I was silent as I took in this bit of casually delivered information. This was a new one for me. The girls I'd previously dated
had nothing but contempt for their former lovers. And here was
Chloe telling me that she was still on friendly terms with the man
who had torn these panties from her ass and fucked her—fucked
her so expertly, in fact, that she was still blushing at the mere
thought of him. My heart was thumping fiercely, and I realized I
was clenching my teeth as well as my fists. I breathed deeply and
exhaled slowly, trying to get control of the unusual emotions that
were flooding through me. I looked up at Chloe—with her snug-
fitting T-shirt stretched across her pert, braless breasts and her

pale pink, French-cut cotton briefs hugging her ass like a second skin—and I felt another, more familiar feeling swirl within me. A series of erotic images began to flood my brain: all of them showing another man making love to my girlfriend, covering her alabaster skin with greedy kisses, and making her come over and over again as she shivered with ecstasy.

I glanced at the panties scattered across the floor, and as betrayed as I felt by these tokens of another man's lust, I couldn't halt my burgeoning erection. My possessiveness was quickly being tempered by the rapid-fire snapshots that were ricocheting through my head. Jealousy and lust were combining to form a wickedly powerful aphrodisiac. Before long, my hard-on was throbbing painfully in my pants, and I was past the point of trying to understand why these thoughts were turning me on. Seconds ago, I was nearly enraged at the thought of someone else buying her lingerie. Now, all I wanted was to see another man strip off her pretty panties and screw her senseless. I was overwhelmed by the need to bury myself inside her soft, wet pussy even as I pictured another man doing the same.

Chloe finally broke the uncomfortable silence. "Everything okay?" Her brow was furrowed with concern and her emerald green eyes were filled with worry. She was clearly expecting a full-blown tantrum, but it was my turn to surprise her.

"Yeah," I said, eyeing her up and down. My undeniable hunger must've been written all over my face because she immediately relaxed and flashed me a sexy smile that only grew wider when I tossed the panties to the floor, closed the space between us, and took her in my arms.

I pressed my lips to hers, feeling the tension that had developed between us during her panty confession completely dissolve. I grabbed one of her pigtails and pulled her head to the side, exposing her porcelain neck. She gasped in surprise, the sound becoming a groan as my lips skidded across her cheek and down her throat. Standing on her tiptoes, Chloe ground her panty-covered mound against the bulge in my jeans, and I bucked my hips against her body as I drew my mouth upward and kissed along her jaw until my lips were at her ear.

"Tell me, Chloe," I said, as I slipped a finger under the elastic band that was stretched across her right asscheek. "How did James fuck you when you wore these panties?" I snapped the stretchy cotton against her butt, making her jump.

"What?"

"How did he fuck you?" I repeated, running my hands over her body until I was cupping her breasts. Whether from lust or friction, her nipples were poking out in bas-relief against her petal pink shirt. I took her pebble-sized nubs between my fingers and thumbs and tweaked them through her baby tee until her lips parted in a wordless moan. "Did he pull them to the side and finger your little hole? Or did he eat your pussy through this soft cotton?" I asked my last question as I dragged my finger along the length of her slit, but when she pushed down against my finger, I pulled my hand away. Her face scrunched up in petulant disappointment, nearly making me laugh.

"No, you don't get any more until you talk," I said, in a voice that sounded far more calm and collected than I actually felt inside. I was nearly delirious with lust, but I wanted to maintain my control of the situation—and Chloe.

My girlfriend wiggled closer to me, but I moved away and shook my head. That's when she knew I was serious. Her eyes grew wide and her cheeks turned cherry red. She turned her head away before she spoke. Her shyness made my cock throb even harder.

"He'd—he'd spank me." Then she added in a whisper, "He

liked to make my ass match my panties before he'd let me have his cock."

I swallowed the chuckle that threatened to escape my lips. I was liking James more by the second.

"How? How'd he spank you?"

"He'd sit on the sofa and take me over his knee," Chloe said to the floor. I pictured a mystery man spanking my girl's ass until she begged him to make her come, and I'd never dreamt of anything hotter.

Taking Chloe by the hand, I led her to the couch and sat down. Without a word, she draped herself across my lap with an ease that surprised me—and made by cock ache. I'd had a growing suspicion that she had submissive tendencies from the way she'd raise her hands over her head and clutch the rails of my brass headboard when I fucked her. But as she wriggled in my lap, I realized I had a hot little baby slave on my hands.

"Was it on the bare ass, Chloe?"

"Yes, sir," she answered in a tiny voice that made my pulse race.

I slipped two fingers into the wide waistband of her panties and peeled them off her ass. She raised her hips to help me, giving me a perfect view of her pink pussy lips that were already glistening with the evidence of her arousal. Struggling to resist fingering her, I slid the undies down until they were banded around her thighs, wanting them close by for comparison with her soon-to-be blushing bottom.

Chloe's skin is so fair, I knew it wouldn't take very many swats of my hand to turn her snow white bottom a pretty shade of pink, so I was determined to take my time and enjoy the moment. I started with a soft slap that hit dead center on the lower part of her fine cheeks, and Chloe let out a moan of satisfaction.

"You're such a bad girl. Letting all sorts of men take down your panties and spank you," I lectured as my hand connected with her bottom.

"Oh, yes," she sighed, struggling enticingly against my erection in a way that threatened to make me come. I moved her a bit to get myself out of the danger zone and slapped her harshly in the same exact location. This time, her groan was more desperate sounding but still seriously laced with lust.

I knew the sensations from each swat were reverberating in her cunt. Having found her sweet spot, I delivered a half-dozen slaps to the underside of her bottom, right above her aroused pussy, noting how much she squirmed with delight and how her pigtails bounced. On another day, I'd instruct her on the proper way to behave when she's being punished, but I was too hot for her at that moment to care about her lack of decorum. My plans for a slow, deliberate session went out the window, and I picked up the pace of the spanking, my cock desperate to be buried inside her. Every time I slapped her ass, she bucked toward my hard-on, making me swear under my breath and strike her even harder the next time. As she moaned and wriggled, I wondered how often James had spanked her, and if he'd bought her panties in a range of pinks and reds to complement his many dominant moods. And as handprints blossomed on her bottom to form a cock-stiffening shade of pink, I found myself longing to search her panty piles for the dark red ones I'd tossed aside. But it wasn't right to change the rules in the middle of the game. Her heart-shaped ass did indeed match her rose-petal pink panties, which meant only one thing: It was time to fuck.

Breathless, I dragged my hand across her cheeks and enjoyed the subtle heat that radiated from her skin. Chloe had ceased her wiggling and was now raising her ass up toward my hand. I slipped my fingers down her crack and continued moving lower until I grazed her glistening sex. She was deliciously wet. I teased her slit with a single fingertip, and she groaned loudly when I skidded over her puffy clit, which was peeking out of her slick folds.

I was already anticipating sinking my cock between her warm, wet pussy lips, but I wanted Chloe to keep talking. "And once your bottom was perfectly pink, what did James do next?" I asked.

"Oh!" Chloe gasped. She'd fallen so far into sub space that she'd forgotten our little game. "He'd bend me over the back of the sofa, so he could look at my ass while he fucked me," she whispered shyly. With that, I eased her off my lap and positioned her on her knees. I pulled the panties down so that they were lower on her thighs, but still framing her blushing bottom. Chloe gripped the back of the couch and looked back at me over her shoulder. Her eyes were alight with lust as she watched me strip out of my jeans and sidle up to her.

"Did he tease you with his cock?" I asked, tracing my dick along her wet slit. "Or did he give it to you hard and fast?" I plunged inside her harshly; she was luxuriously wet and I slid in to the hilt.

"Hard!" She gasped as she lurched back toward me, her plush cheeks crashing against my pelvis. The sexy warmth of her spanked bottom was irresistible, and I ground my hips against her to savor the heat before pulling out and slamming into her over and over again. Her bunched-up panties were stretched tautly across her thighs, and my tightening balls grazed the band of cotton each time I thrust in and out, urging me toward orgasm.

As Chloe whimpered beneath me, I began to fantasize about me and James taking turns spanking her upturned bottom, and then filling her pussy and mouth with cock as she bucked excitedly between us. That dirty daydream made it easy to answer my girlfriend's demands of "Harder—faster!" I plunged my dick into her soft, wet tunnel as I thought of how many pairs of panties surrounded us and how many sex games she and James had played together. But by that point, my jealousy had entirely dissipated and morphed into an endless kaleidoscope of possibilities.

Chloe's cries were accelerating in volume and pitch and called me back to the very sexy present. I reached a hand underneath her, stroking one of her breasts through her T-shirt and running my fingers down her torso toward her pussy. I sought out her clit, rubbing her button with two fingertips in the way I know she likes best. My circling fingers did their best to stay on target as she bounced around and fucked herself on my dick. Her rhythmic cries soon joined together in one long, keening moan as she came, her sex clutching my shaft and sending me tumbling into oblivion mere seconds after she did. I collapsed on the couch with Chloe in my arms, smiling as I savored my first orgasm that was delivered—however indirectly—by another man.

I helped Chloe straighten up her place that day, insisting that she keep every last scrap of silk and lace. I'm many things, but I'm not wasteful. After sex like that, it seemed wrong to let a single pair go. I'd only begun to discover the joy that could be found in her dresser drawers and looked forward to adding to her collection of memories.

As I headed out the door that night, I turned back to her to offer a hint of the wicked scheme that was playing in my head. "Invite James over to have dinner with us next week—I'll bring the panties."

BACK WHEN

A. Silenus

Trevor had a number of regrets, and one of them was that he had never had an orgasm in transit. He'd heard, or perhaps he'd read somewhere, that there was nothing more delicious than experiencing the glowing eruption of semen into a receptive mouth while driving.

Without even glancing at his passenger, however, he knew there was more chance of his lottery number being announced on the car radio. His wife was just not the kind of woman to risk cum breath on the way to a family wedding.

About the only thing remotely exotic about her, as Trevor saw it, was her name, Ceadora—bestowed by an alcoholic mother who couldn't quite remember the name of that actress, or was it a writer. You know, the one who got garroted by her scarf in an open-top car.

Trussed in her dark plum suit, as she was now, with a bouquet of white ruffles from her blouse sprouting around the neck, Ceadora was all business and not much for spontaneous pleasure. Even when they'd met, in their midthirties, she'd been career focused. Settling down had taken her a few years, she told him, and she had some catching up to do jobwise. And that was all the response he got to his ever more obtuse and despondent entreaties for more playtime.

But while her vermilion lips said "No," in so many words, and her painstakingly made-up face flashed a clear anti-hanky-panky warning, the fact that her hips, waist, and bosom still undulated in all the right places was enough to make a man—even her husband—ponder the potential.

He was musing along these lines, paying only slightly more attention to the road than if Madonna had just called on his cell phone, when Ceadora's commanding tone brought him back to reality. He recognized their locality almost instantly. This was his wife's old neighborhood, a few blocks from the church where her niece was due to marry, the same building in fact where their own ceremony had occurred all those years ago.

Ceadora announced that she had a few last-minute purchases to make and directed him into a parking lot at a strip mall. Vacant spots were few, but Trevor eventually slotted into one outside a bar. His wife glanced uneasily at a gaggle of clients on the sidewalk taking a break from thirst quenching.

"Well, it will have to do," she said. "Now don't go far. I won't be long."

He watched, as did the loitering clientele, while Ceadora strutted across the asphalt as erect and controlled as a stilt walker. Briefly he considered his options. Then he sauntered toward neon beer signs and the opportunity for reflection before the family's rendezvous with one of life's milestones.

Low lighting and piped music quickly shrank his universe to a dark wooden counter, a barmaid's compressed bosom zipping across his field of vision with the consistency of a typewriter carriage (remember those?), and a bottle of some microbrew that actually possessed both aroma and flavor. At least two senses will have a day to remember, he decided. That was some consolation.

Gradually he became aware of conversation seeping across the room.

"It's her, all right," said a man built like an oil drum on the stool next to him. "I'd know that walk anywhere."

"That hair was a giveaway," agreed a guy in checkered shirt and jeans leaning on the counter just beyond. "Not the same without those skimpy outfits she used to wear but still has a taste for flashy jewelry by the look of it."

"Wonder what she's doing here," mused a third as he stretched across the pool table for a long shot.

For the first time the trio directed their attention Trevor's way.

"She used to be quite a celebrity around here," the heavyset one elaborated, drawing Trevor into the discussion the way semi-inebriated regulars sometimes do when they notice a stranger in their midst.

"Well known and well loved," echoed an endorsement off the green baize.

For a moment Trevor could do little more than grin, the way strangers do when trying to ingratiate themselves with newfound buddies they don't necessarily want. He looked around for the lady in question, but the only one remotely in evidence was the barmaid clinking around among crates in some back room.

"Who, who is this you're talking about?" he faltered eventually.

"The broad outside just now, in the purple," rumbled the oil drum. "You passed her as you came in, didn't you?"

"Life of the party on more than one occasion," the pool player went on to explain.

"On that very table on one occasion, as I recall," joined in the guy in the checkered shirt, and the three of them broke into a clatter of whoops and cackles.

"Lost a wager on a game, didn't she?" he continued. "Something about loser has to do what winner wants."

"No, you got it wrong, Gary," smirked the one on the stool. "She won the wager."

More laughter and then more from Gary.

"You could be right. All I remember is her—what was her name now?—with four of us stretching her out across this table and tying her wrists, and this big hulking guy she used to like peeling off her bra and panties. She was loving it, I swear. Giggling like a schoolgirl...Wish I could remember her name. Something short and sweet. Dora maybe."

Trevor tried to imagine his wife giggling like a schoolgirl. That was as far as his imagination would take him. Ripples of derision were more her style. Giggling must have come before his time.

Gary turned stiffly toward his friend on the stool as another mental picture came into focus.

"Hey, John, remember when they had the mechanical bull in here?"

"Oh, god, that's a thought."

John was evidently getting as much of a kick from explaining to Trevor as he was out of the memory itself.

"See, she had her own way of riding that thing. She wasn't lookin' for a rough ride. No, she had 'em slow it down, and then she'd rub that cute little ass of hers up and down it like she had some pelvic itch she couldn't quite reach."

Gary couldn't resist cutting in.

"That's exactly what she did have," he said, and the laughter gurgled out of all three until he regained enough control to continue. " 'Specially when she found someone to share the ride. Remember that bartender she fancied, and how she got him up there with her?"

"Yeah, didn't she wrap her legs around that one?" the pool player broke in. "Between the two of them they put quite a shine on that old bull."

"She was moanin' and squirmin' like it was that bull inside her," Gary remembered. "Guys were climbin' up there just to squeeze her buns. Like maybe they could get an orgasm just from contact."

Could they be talking about the same woman, Trevor wondered. That reverberating tone of Ceadora's always seemed so unshakable. The notion of it melting into a helpless soliloquy of lust and surrender was an improbable dream.

There was a lull as smiles faded into sighs, and then John turned toward Trevor.

"Hey, friend, forgive us. We're probably boring you stupid with all this talk 'bout some little fox you never had a chance to appreciate."

"Yeah, too bad for you," came the coda from Gary.

Just then there was a flash as the door swung open, and Trevor saw a familiar silhouette outlined against the invading daylight.

"There you are, Trevor. Let's go," she instructed him. "Time's going by."

He followed on her heels with a murmured good-bye to anyone who was still listening. Not that anyone was. It was all the trio could do to stare. What he would have given to be there if they ever recovered the gifts of speech and movement.

"Some of the regulars felt they might have known you," he mumbled as they drove away. "Swore you used to be quite a popular fixture there."

"That's absurd," she said.

"That's what I thought."

He replied without hesitation, mimicking her own way of brushing off the unthinkable—or, at least, setting limits for what others might think. What would be the point of doing otherwise? It was all so long ago, and so out of reach.

In all the years they had been together she had never once intimated that she would welcome a barroom brawl with multiple play partners. He'd long given up hinting about ropes and other restraints. Her rejections had come in the form of a terse change of subject or, if pressed, a fluttering laugh that always left him wondering whether it was the idea or him that was the point of the rebuff.

She was right. It was all so absurd.

For once they were in sync.

POPSICLE IN THE LIBRARY

Zaedryn Meade

You know there's no food allowed in the library," I growl in her ear, pressing her stomach against the concrete stairwell wall. I'm speaking quietly but it still echoes.

She groans, not able to form words, mouth open.

"Not very polite of you, breaking the rules like that." I lift her dress and shove my hands under the edge of her panties. She's wet. "Oh, you like this, do you? You're enjoying this?" I flick my fingers over her cunt, then pull my hand away. She whimpers, echoing in the stairwell.

"You want something to suck on, girl, you take this," and I let up on the pressure against her. She peels her cheek away from the concrete. I take my hand from her hair and unzip my fly, pull out my packing cock, bend it straight. "Go on, suck it."

She drops to her knees, lips red from the cherry Popsicle she'd been sucking lewdly when I walked up to her. And here I'd thought we had a study date. Her legs were all long in the windowsill, summery dress light and airy, and when she moved her knees I could see the thin cream fabric covering her pussy, the outline of her lips, plump, thick.

She'd offered the sweet, bright red Popsicle to me. "Want some?" Eyes all sly and sparkly, playful smile on her mouth.

I had shaken my head no. Crossed my arms over my chest. Raised one eyebrow and nodded for her to continue. She did. Slid the whole thing into her mouth and got cherry juice on her chin.

And now she sucks me just like she was working that sticky treat a moment ago, sucking it like she could pull the juice from me too, like she could use the muscles in her cheeks to draw the cum from me and swallow it all.

Fuck. I want her to make me shoot in her mouth like that. Oh, I wish I could.

"Enough," I say and pull her to her feet. I don't take her panties off, just lift her dress and finger the fleshy parts of her ass with my hand, then give it a good smack.

Not too hard. I cup my palm a little bit and it echoes perfectly, which makes the slight sting more impressive because it sounds so loud. I smack again. She cries out a little. Again, harder, and she yelps, I hear it floors away. My cock is still out and I shove it into her. Hard. Slide it in all the way. She whimpers; presses her hands into the concrete, the side of her face; presses her ass into me, spreads her legs.

She actually shouts, my thrusts pounding the noise out of her.

"Quiet," I say, harsh, in her ear.

She is still whimpering, trying to be quiet, and she whispers, "I'm gonna come if you keep fucking me like that."

"Oh, yeah? Bring it on, bitch. Come on, come for me." My mouth at her ear and my hands on her hips, head of my cock hitting her G-spot, I can feel it, and she comes hard, wet, dripping; soaking my cock, her thighs, the floor, my shoes. Her body shudders but that's not all I can get out of her, and I pull out and twist her around before she's regained her composure, slide my fingers in, slide my hand in, reach up and inside her, and I can feel the spots to press and I do.

"Do it again." She shakes her head no but she's gasping, legs wide and on her tiptoes on the wet floor. She grabs for my wrist to pull me back, embarrassment in her eyes, and she can feel her own cum dripping down her legs, but I don't let up.

I take hold of her hair with my other hand and pull her head back, press my mouth to her jaw, saying, "You're going to come just for me."

And she wraps her arms around my neck and comes, and comes, and comes.

MORNING, NOON, AND NIGHT

Alison Tyler

Marriage changes everything," Naomi told her assistant.

"Everything?" Vanessa asked, looking up from her usual spot on the lipstick red sofa. She'd been organizing Naomi's tiny electronic date book, her fingers expertly working the miniscule keyboard. Now, she paused midkey to stare at her dark-haired boss, who clearly craved the full attention of her audience of one. Over the two years she'd worked as Naomi's personal assistant, Vanessa had come to recognize the silent signs in her boss's gestures and posture; the way the woman's voice changed, the way she paced. She could have written a manual called Decoding Naomi.

Now, Naomi strode forcefully in her four-inch heels from her stark white desk to the window, then stared out at the clear sky. Or maybe she wasn't staring at the sky, Vanessa realized. She was admiring her own reflection, darting her tongue out over her top lip, before tossing her glossy black hair off her shoulders with a trademark flick of her head. She looked good for forty, Vanessa thought, but she had a lot of help.

While Naomi stared at herself, Vanessa gazed out the floor-to-ceiling window. The office featured a view of the rolling hills, which Vanessa always thought was ironic because Naomi's mansion, perched up in the hills, boasted a city view that included her office.

"Women change. *Men* change."

"Men?"

"Well, husbands."

She spoke from experience. Naomi had married young. At nineteen, she'd married for love, but had gotten money as a bonus, wedding a rich boy seven years her senior who had come with wealth, and who'd turned that inheritance into a fortune. Vanessa knew her boss's history, had seen the framed wedding invitation on the wall of her mansion, right above the invite to Naomi and Dean's china anniversary party, which she'd helped organize the year before.

But even though her boss had been married more than twenty years, Vanessa didn't believe the woman had anything viable to offer in the advice department. Yet she couldn't let her true feelings show on her face. With a sigh, Vanessa set the date book on her lap, and then spun her engagement ring slowly around her finger while wondering whether or not to let Naomi continue. Vanessa knew her boss was having an affair, and she guessed that Naomi's husband was, as well. As the all-knowing keeper of Naomi's appointment book, Vanessa had the older woman's schedule memorized. From her thrice weekly visits to Jose Eber to the mani and pedi every Friday afternoon, to the "Pilates appointments" on Wednesdays that were really glorified fuck sessions with her lover Neil.

Dean's affairs were less obvious, but Vanessa had strong feelings about them anyway. She knew because Dean would call to check Naomi's whereabouts, and the guilt in his voice made it apparent to her why he was checking.

"Men change," Naomi said again, and Vanessa wanted to say, "Not *my* man," but couldn't. She hadn't been hired to have an opinion. She guessed that her even temper, quiet façade, and unshakeable demeanor were what Naomi appreciated most about her. Naomi liked the way Vanessa had her life organized. Compartmentalized. Condoms for her lover. Diaphragm for her husband. Sex with Neil every Wednesday. Sex with Dean Tuesday, Thursday, and Sunday mornings.

That's not how it was with Vanessa and Kerry.

They fucked morning, noon, and night.

What her boss didn't understand was that Vanessa knew Naomi's schedule so well because Kerry liked to screw her on Naomi's desk. He would call to make sure Naomi was away from the office at one appointment or another—not caring whether she was being painted, plucked, waxed, or fucked, only that she was off in her shiny red Beamer for at least the half hour he could sneak away from his own work. One thing was for sure, his voice held none of the guilt that Naomi's husband's did. Instead, Kerry's baritone contained that low throb of impending climax, that desire to see Vanessa naked and spread out on her boss's desk. A desk she was responsible for wiping down every evening. Naomi liked things neat, while Kerry liked to put Vanessa's feet up on his shoulders. He insisted Naomi had bought a desk this high for him, the perfect height for him to fuck his future wife.

"She knows," he had said once.

Vanessa shook her head, her blonde curls spreading out on the smooth cool desk.

"She knows what a dirty little slut you are," he'd insisted, "and that's why she hired you. To live vicariously through your sex life."

"She's plenty busy enough on her own," Vanessa had countered.

"What? With her *Pilates* man?" Kerry couldn't say the word *Pilates* without sneering.

Vanessa had chuckled. She'd met the instructor before. Neil was well-built, mechanically tan, and attractive in a Ken doll sort of way, but she believed that he fucked several of the wealthy Beverly Hills wives. That was his job. At least, that's how he made his money.

"Just look at her," Kerry insisted, pointing to the glamour shot of Naomi that hung on her wall, a picture she used for the back cover of the best-selling romance novels she wrote. A picture that resembled her only in theory, since it was airbrushed to the point of mirror smoothness. She was smooth in person, too, thanks to thrice yearly Botox injections. But nobody had totally poreless skin like the woman in the picture on her wall.

As if on cue, as Vanessa's cheeks flushed and her body was primed to climax, the phone rang. Kerry didn't stop fucking her, but she had to twist at the waist to lean over, pressing the blinking button as she lifted the receiver, and answering with a breathless, "Naomi Miller's office, how can I help you?"

In this new position, with one leg crossed over the other, the pleasure of Kerry's cock inside her intensified. The fact that he worked one hand between her thighs to flick her clit made her nearly breathless.

"Is she there?"

It was her husband. Dean was a lawyer. When he called, she always felt as if she were on the witness stand.

"No, she's coming—" Christ, *Vanessa* was so on the verge of coming, she'd said the wrong thing. Naomi was going. But *where* was she going? The sweet burst of pleasure was making her head spin. "She's going to Pilates this afternoon."

"Oh, that's right," he said, the same way he did nearly every week. There was a sigh of relief in his voice that made Vanessa sure he was off to some tryst of his own. Did he do his secretary while Naomi screwed the Pilates man? Or was he more discreet than that, choosing pay-by-the-hour models? Maybe Mr. Miller fucked his masseuse—or was fucked by his masseur. Vanessa didn't know. She didn't really care in more than an offhandedly curious way. All she was sure of was that she had to get off the phone quickly, before Kerry made her scream.

"Thanks, Vanessa."

She was hanging up the phone when he continued, and she had to scramble to get the receiver to her ear again. "Oh, and I forgot to mention, kid. Congratulations."

Was he giving her props for fucking her man at work? She shuddered as she felt the very start of the orgasm begin to work through her, those flutters in the base of her belly radiating upward and outward. As she put one hand up to her mouth, intent on covering her heavy breathing, she saw the diamond engagement ring flash.

"Thank you, sir," she said to two men at once.

Kerry hung the phone up for her, and then gripped her hips and pulled her down hard on him. When he ran one thumb along her clit a final time, she could hold back no longer. The heat flared through her, and she threw her head back and came, staring at the portrait—now seen upside down from her position—of her boss on the wall.

Less than ten miles away, in a suite at the Beverly Hills Hotel, Dean had his wife bent over the edge of the bed.

"You like me to talk to her when she's fucking her boyfriend, don't you, babe?"

"Fiancé," she corrected him. "They got engaged on Valentine's Day."

"Whatever," Dean murmured, hands in his wife's thick dark hair. He loved how soft her hair was, loved the smell of it. He could get hard imagining Naomi's hairdresser brushing her shoulder-length tresses. This was why he asked her to go to the salon so often. He didn't care if Patrick was gay. The thought of another man playing with Naomi's hair always turned him on. "You know, she thinks you're doing the Pilates man."

"What a pussy."

"Vanessa?"

"No, Neil. Ponytail-sporting geek. I know Linda's fucking him, but damn. That woman has no taste."

"Speaking of taste," Dean grinned, then flipped her over and began to eat her pussy, her legs over his shoulders. He loved dining on her after he'd come inside of her. Naomi tightened her long, lean thighs around him as he flicked his tongue over her clit.

While her husband traced circles over her mound, Naomi put her arms above her head and gripped her wrists, as if she'd been cuffed. As Dean's tongue spiraled over her clit, she thought about the conversation she'd had with Vanessa earlier in the day. She'd tried to tell Vanessa about marriage, but she hadn't done a good job, she thought now.

She had wanted to share her secrets. To explain. Men changed. Women changed. You had to constantly keep things moving, create your own excitement. This was the reason why she and Dean cheated with each other in the middle of the week. An elaborate scheme, perhaps, but she knew that the setup allowed her to experience her husband in an illicit sort of way. And leaving her office so often also gave Vanessa and Kerry the time they needed to fuck on her desk, which both she and Dean found erotic. Sometimes they'd go to the office at night, and Dean would be Kerry and she would be Vanessa. Sometimes, she'd bring a strap-on and *she* would be Kerry and *he* would be Vanessa.

That's what she had wanted to tell Vanessa, without really telling her. Naomi had wanted to explain that creating a good, solid marriage was a lot of work. That the energy and excitement young lovers took for granted could last well into the future, but you had to be willing to make an effort.

Dean was always willing. Recently, he had suggested they get one of those little nanny cams to post in the office. That way, they could watch Vanessa and Kerry at their leisure, reclining at home in their million-dollar mansion, on the flat-screen TV mounted across from their bed. They hadn't done that yet, but the concept excited her.

She'd wanted to tell Vanessa a lot—but maybe these were lessons you needed to learn for yourself.

Marriage changes things, Naomi thought to herself as Dean's tongue crested her clit and she started to come. But she and Dean had never let that fact stop them from doing it morning, noon, and night.

WELCOME TO THE NEIGHBORHOOD

Ariel Graham

Paige leaned against the front porch rails, stretching her legs and hoping to get her breath back. It had only been a short run around her high Sierra neighborhood but the day was really windy and her entire run back to the house had been straight into the wind. She was hot, sweaty, and covered in wind-blown dust that was quickly trying to turn into mud, and when she looked up she locked eyes with her new neighbor.

Oh, terrific—because Nicki was taller than Paige, with naturally white-blonde hair cropped short, big brown eyes, muscles like an off-season bodybuilder's, no body fat, and she always looked like she'd just stepped out of a salon.

Paige looked like she'd just stepped out of a tornado. But she grinned sheepishly, and waved, and only winced inwardly when Nicki called, "Hey, my phone hasn't been turned on yet, and my cell is on the fritz. Can I use yours?"

Cell or home phone? Paige wondered, and then called, "Let me bring it over," which would give her a minute to wash her face and at least put on mascara.

Nicki was far too nice to put her out like that. She jumped neatly over the eighteen-inch decorative fence between their yards and jogged up the steps wearing flat tennies without laces and a little black sports dress. She looked totally put together. "Don't bother, I can use it here if that's all right."

Feeling like the "before" picture in a makeover article, Paige nodded, handed her phone over from the runner's pouch Velcro'd around her upper arm, and indicated she'd be right back. She left the front door open, uncertain what the etiquette was when your neighbor was making a phone call on your cell on your front porch and you wanted to go wash your face while she did so in order to stop looking tornado stricken.

She washed her face in the hall bathroom with the door open and she could just hear Nicki out on the porch. She ran her hands through her unruly red curls and decided they weren't going to improve without serious work, found an old tube of mascara in her purse, and finally gave up on the whole thing just before Nicki knocked on the open front door.

"They claim I never put in an order for phone service," she said, handing Paige her phone back. "And this seems to make sense to them. Don't most people still have landlines as well as cells?"

"Especially up here where cell service comes and goes," Paige said, pocketing the phone. She was starting to ask, "Do you want to come in for some—" and racking her brain as to what liquids they had in the house when Nicki interrupted her thoughts.

"Thanks again. I've got to run. Got a job interview this afternoon." She jumped off the porch like an eight-year-old, waved, cleared the fence, and was gone.

Paul got home early. From the kitchen, she heard him on the porch calling something to Nicki and heard her laugh in response. Then he came in, bringing summer heat and looking tall and sandy and gorgeous. He brought with him wine and grapes and bread and a fancy sheep's milk cheese she could never quite manage the name of.

"What's the occasion?" He was usually home late. When she'd married an architect, she hadn't expected him to be so tired every night, but after fifteen years of marriage he was coming home and conking out in the recliner and complaining when she forced him up and onto the treadmill, even though he'd asked her to nag him.

"Finished the project on that bank building downtown," he said. He opened the wine with a skill that always annoyed her a little, since opening wine was hit or miss for her. "Now it's in the hands of the contractors." He put down the wine, put his arms around her and kissed her neck between ear and shoulder. "I am a free man."

"You are a dreamer," she laughed. "Now begin the calls from the general, the subs, the owners, the—mmm—what are you doing?"

He'd abandoned the wine and cheese and his lips were slipping from her neck to her collarbone and down into the scoop of the sundress she'd put on after her shower. "You let me fantasize my way and I'll indulge yours," he said, and added, "I saw Nicki on the porch. You're right, she is hot." And to take away any potential sting, his hands slid down from her waist to her hips and around to her ass and he pulled her tight against him. Under his jeans, he was hard.

She ran her hands along his arms, over the chambray work shirt, loving the cinnamon smell of his skin from being outside on a job site in the sun.

He let her go, kissed her forehead, poured two glasses of wine, and turned toward the bedroom. She stopped to lock the front door, but he handed her the wine and said, "I'll get the door; be right behind you," and she went up the hall with the wine, into the late afternoon shade-dappled bedroom still warm with summer heat.

The wine went on the bedside table. His shirt went down on the floor. She loved it when he held her against his hard, hot chest and still wore his jeans. Her dress followed his shirt and he grinned. She'd neglected to put on underwear. Paige's skin was creamy white, lightly freckled from countless careless encounters with summer sunshine. Paul ran his hands down her sides again, along her ass, over the hips she despaired of. Paige was curvier than she wanted to be, with heavy creamy breasts. He nuzzled them and she stepped back toward the bed. Paul got there first, and pulled her down on top of him, their legs wrapped around each other. His hands stroked her shoulders and back. He leaned up, kissing her throat. "Tell me that fantasy again," he whispered.

She whispered back, "Don't stop kissing me."

He brushed her curls back and she relaxed into the feel of his hands, stroking, kneading, pressing against her ass, pulling her close. He moved one leg between hers, pressing against her wet pussy, and she pushed against him, her own hands holding his shoulders, his arms, touching his hair. She closed her eyes and imagined again.

"We're like this. It's hot and the blinds are open a little, and our bodies are hot and slick together. We've got wine and there's nothing we have to do and nothing to hurry for."

She paused, caught his mouth with hers. His tongue tasted of wine, oaky and red. She pressed into his mouth, felt his lips suck at her tongue. Her hands spread across his chest, stroking, sinking lower.

"You're very hard," she said. "I can feel the wet on the head

as I slide my body down yours, kissing your chest—like this—
and like this—and playing with your cock."

She stopped talking again and gave a long, slow lap up the
length of his cock, then sucked the head into her mouth, savoring
the salty precum, the musky heat of him where he'd worked all
of a summer's day in jeans. She sucked his balls one at a time
into her mouth, then returned to his cock, sliding as much of his
length and thickness into her mouth as she could.

Paul groaned and shifted, his hands in her hair.

"Then you pull me up to you, kissing me," she broke off,
laughing in her throat, as his mouth covered hers and his tongue
touched her lips, brushing hers gently. He nibbled her lower lip
and released it.

"And you pull me up so I'm straddling your face, my hands
against the headboard and your—oh—"

His mouth came up against her pussy, his tongue unerringly
finding her clit, and he began lapping and nibbling, his hands
stroking between her legs, spreading her wetness, moving just
around her lips, just at the edge of her ass, until she began to
shudder, and he moved to form a seal with his mouth and to
send his tongue as deep into her as he could.

Her body throbbed to the heartbeat of her orgasm, rings of
pleasure radiating until she relaxed against him, slid down his
body to straddle his hips, his cock pressed hard against her cunt
and clit but not yet sliding inside.

"You haven't entered me yet and we're both so hot, waiting,
pressing against each other with me on top and then there's this
shadow, just a hint of someone there. She touches my shoulder
with her hand and I don't need to look, I know it's Nicki. The bed
dips as she climbs on behind me and her hands run over my back,
down to my waist, back up. They come around and she starts to
touch my breasts, squeezing them, playing with my nipples, and

I feel something strange, hard, cold, then I'm kissing you and she's kissing the back of my neck. You move, shift your hips, and your cock slides up inside me. And she moves and she's wearing a strap-on and it slides up into my ass, and we start to move as if we've done this a hundred times before, Nicki and you taking up a rhythm and what she's wearing rubs her clit with every stroke so she's groaning, her breasts pressed against my back, the three of us moving to your rhythm as you move faster."

She leaned down to kiss him, her hands stroking his cock, meaning to turn fantasy to reality. He was hard and huge tonight, rigid, his breath uneven as he drove his cock into her pussy. His eyes were full of light, still teasing, almost laughing, but he was too distracted to speak, his eyes tracking something over her shoulder.

"What?" she almost asked.

And Nicki's hand touched her shoulder.

DISCO QUEEN

Sommer Marsden

W ould you look at this?" Dan held the swingy pale yellow
garment up and spun in a circle.

"I'm sure it will look lovely on you," Keely said. She attempted
to catch a stack of magazines as they slid to the side, but failed.
She stepped back as the periodicals continued to spread.

"What are we looking for again?" Dan sighed. But then he
was laughing because the garage was stifling and his wife looked
like she would start cussing up a blue streak at any moment.

"We are looking for Nana Retha's quilt set. Mom said I could
have it. She also assured me it was out here. And what *is* that?"

"This old thing?" Dan teased, twirling again and clutching
the pale yellow dress to his broad chest.

"Let me see that."

Dan tossed her the dress and she held it up. *Circa 1971 easy*,
Keely thought. "Wow. Vintage. Am I right? Mom must have
been wearing this right before she got pregnant with me." It
was her turn to hold up the dress and primp. Little puffs of dust

came off the fabric and she sneezed and then sneezed again.

"You know, I think you'd look pretty sexy in that disco queen number," Dan said. "I can see it now. A little Bee Gees blasting from the stereo and some strappy heels. You could definitely pull it off."

Keely snorted, but studied the pale yellow wrap dress again. She probably *would* fill it out pretty well. And the dress would make a hell of a costume for a Halloween party. But in the middle of a June heat wave Halloween seemed a million miles away. Plus, she was pretty sure that she saw her grandmother's quilt peeking out from an ancient cedar chest in the corner. She tossed the dress to Dan and said, "Yeah, yeah, jive talking. I see the quilt."

She took off for the corner, barely paying attention when Dan said, "I think I just found a strobe light. Staying alive, baby."

Dan had Wednesdays off. Keely did not. She dragged her ass home through the heat hoping that her man would have two things for her: an ice-cold Corona with extra lime and some plan for dinner. She was hungry, thirsty, tired, and hot. Not a good combination. She parked under the oak hoping the tree would keep the interior of her car a bit cooler, then she walked barefoot up the stone path to the front door, her two-inch work heels tucked under her arm. She opened the front door to a luscious blast of air-conditioning and something else. A strange sound. A steady thumping bass with some high-pitched melody. And then she recognized the high soprano of Barry Gibb.

"Oh, you are fucking kidding me," she said to herself and then started laughing. On the sofa lay the yellow disco dress on a wire dry cleaners hanger. A note was propped on the bodice. WEAR ME. On the floor was a pair of gold strappy vintage heels. Something straight out of *Saturday Night Fever.* PUT ME ON, that note ordered.

Keely dropped her shoes and shut the door. Although still hot and tired, she felt suddenly a bit renewed to see how Dan had spent his day. Clearly, he'd been preparing an interesting homecoming for her. Better than a beer and a burger. After slipping her silk skirt down, she kicked it off. Next went her white cotton shell top. When she reached for the dress, the note that said WEAR ME toppled forward and under sat another card. This one was marked: NO PANTIES, PLEASE.

She laughed softly in the golden-lit room but dropped her small pink drawers. She noticed as she tossed the panties that the crotch was wet. Keely took a deep breath and tried to steady herself as she slid the buttery yellow dress down over her head and cinched the tie a bit tighter around her waist. When she grabbed the shoes, that note fell away and beneath a card read: SORRY, NO BRA EITHER.

Now she was giggling, wrestling with the wrap dress, shucking the bra, her hard nipples spiking against the fabric. The music stopped and anxiety worked through her. Had he thought she was not coming? Had he changed his mind? Shut it down? Dan would wait, wouldn't he?

She strapped the sandals on and smoothed her hair. Just when she thought she might cry from trying to hurry to get to him, the music started up again, another disco hit.

"I never realized how many Bee Gees songs I knew," she whispered to herself as she walked through the kitchen on the high wooden heels. When she opened the basement door, the music seemed to double in volume and bright flashes of light lit the stairwell in a crazy dance of light and dark.

"Dan?" she called when she was halfway down.

The clubbed basement was empty at first glance. The hard

tile floor they loathed so much had been cleared and mopped. A spangled dangling disco ball had been suspended from the drop ceiling. And the strobe light Dan had pilfered from her parents' garage was throwing flashes of hot white light. Then a man unfolded from behind the built-in bar (that they totally intended to tear down), and she snickered before she could catch herself. White suit, black open-throated top, hair slicked back. "May I have this dance, foxy lady?" Dan asked, and Keely laughed at him but her cunt went soft and wet.

"You may. But I warn you, I've got two left feet." She looked down at the vintage shoes, which must have cost a fortune even on eBay and said, "And now I've got two left feet in really big shoes. That's a deadly combination."

Dan danced his way across the floor, pulling his best John Travolta moves all the way. It was something that Keely could not control, the laughter that swelled up and out of her even as she felt a delightful little shiver at how much he clearly wanted to fuck her senseless. His hips were pistoning toward her in a faux fucking motion that made her shoulders shake with giggles. But it was hot too, because she could tell even in the crazy flashing light that made his movements jerky and surreal that his cock was hard. Really hard.

Keely gave in and danced toward him, doing the only move that she could think of—the finger point and hip gyration. "That's it," Dan said and caught her up in his arms, spinning her to the sickening sweet beat and lyrics. He bit her neck lightly and her nipples went hard and tingly all over again. His hands smoothed over her ass, touched the curve of her waist, cupped her breasts. He was every bit the grabby man on the dance floor under the strobe light. His movement somehow seemed half time but yet a faster speed than normal.

Keely felt the wetness between her legs and the steady pulse of a swift and eager want. She wished she could drag him to the sofa and climb on top of him right there. But this was his big thing so she waited.

He bent, still moving to the music, a slower song now. He pushed his hands up under the flared skirt of the dress, pushing it up to her waist as he moved his big hands higher. Then he knelt, right there in his horrible white suit, and she watched him dip his head to taste her. The strobing made it look like he was moving in jerky little motions. When Dan's mouth moved over her clit and he dragged the flat of his tongue over her there, she shut her eyes. All she could see of the lights then were the flashes and shadows they created behind her closed lids.

The music stopped, but the lights did not and Dan licked her pussy until she felt her knees grow soft and an orgasm wrung her out and left her limp. "Please, Dan," she said, knowing that after all this time he would know what she meant.

Dan moved her up against the support pole he always joked was a stripper pole in disguise. He put her hands above her head and whispered into her ear, right up close, "Hold on sweetheart. Keep your hand up, Keely," and then his zipper sounded in the new flashing silence of their ugly clubbed basement. "Spread yourself wider for me, baby."

And she did. Widening her stance on those horribly uncomfortable wooden heels. His cock, warm and hard, nudged at her opening, and she arched back against him, feeling every bit the dance-floor whore she was for the evening. "Fuck me," she said, falling into the fantasy. They were making their own music now, not disco. The steady slap of their fucking, the soft sounds that escaped her even when she didn't know they were coming, the groan low in Dan's throat that meant he was right there and trying not to come.

He gripped her waist as she held the slippery basement

support pole, and when his fingers found her clit and strummed, she came again, his moving hand swirling the yellow dress around her thighs. Dan was right behind her, laughing in her ear when he came. "Goddamn, baby, you look good in that dress. A fantasy come true."

She watched his hands move to hers and pull them down, their jerky white movements in the dark glowing basement. She liked the way his big hands looked wrapped around her small, slim wrists. "I'll get down with you any day," she laughed, but she found that she wanted him all over again.

"Down and dirty?" he quipped.

"I'm ready," Keely said and pushed back against him to show him it was true.

STRAIGHT-LACED

A. D. R. Forte

He's naked. He puts on his boots. They shine like black granite; his old drill sergeant from basic would be proud. He wonders what his sergeant would have thought about his reason for polishing these boots now.

That makes him grin as he ties the laces.

Boots on, he goes to the chair in the middle of the room and straddles it. He sits wrong away 'round, facing the window, and crosses his arms on the back. The chair legs and frame are cold, and the upholstery is rough on naked skin. He watches his stuff dangle in the space between the back and the seat of the chair. He's not erect. Not yet.

He needs to stay that way, so he focuses on the trees outside. Bare, winter trees. Naked and cold, punished by the icy air.

He sighs. Nothing will serve to distract him right now. Anticipation burns much too fiercely. He's learned not to fidget, training is good for that. But his impatience doesn't torment him any less for sitting still. While he waits.

Time that he doesn't—cannot—measure passes in excruciating silence. The clouded-over sky behind the gray, wind-
whipped branches doesn't give him any clues to seconds or hours
or minutes. He takes deep, slow breaths that go all the way to
the pit of his stomach. He feels himself go still, detached from
the cold room and this hard chair.

The trees outside dance soundlessly. He imagines he has
no senses at all: no touch, no smell, nothing but sight. He is
perfectly, utterly empty.

A void waiting to be filled.

The door opens. At once, the hair on the nape of his neck
rises, the muscles in his back tense. Reflex action. Ready for
fight or flight or...a thread of pleasure travels down his spine
and he fights the temptation to imagine. He forces himself to
empty his mind again.

But his senses still strain for movement he can barely hear,
practiced as he is at listening. The sound of her steps as she crosses
the room. The rustle of her clothes as she kneels behind him.

He feels her cold hands.

A chill passes through all his skin. Blood rushes down his
veins, making its way straight to his groin. It's useless to fight
it now. He feels her fingers spreading his cheeks, and her wet
tongue probes and dances between muscle and skin.

This is a surprise, or at least half of one. She isn't predict-
able by any means, but he's come to expect anything. His balls
tighten as her finger slides behind them, moving in circles, and
his dick stiffens obediently. Thankfully.

He thinks that this is the kind of chair you find in church.
He's sat in church before, aching with a nameless, undefined
need. Long before he met her. He thinks over the things she does
to him now and the things he does to her. Things they sure as
hell wouldn't have approved of in church. Things that nobody

who knows him, who ever knew the person he was before her, would approve of.

He could delve into all the complicated, obscure reasons for why that's changed. But he knows it goes deeper than that, like the way she always takes his dick in her mouth as far as she can possibly stand it. Pushing her own limit. She'd have made a good soldier; she never does anything halfway.

It's hard to breathe. As if she's read his mind, she withdraws her fingers and her tongue, and stands. He lifts his head and gulps air.

A shadow falls between him and the window, blocks his vision with white—a slender waist, two small breasts wrapped up tight in a close-fitting, low-cut sweater. He swallows hard.

She kneels, kicking her long skirt out of the way so she can get low enough to reach him, displaying the slope of her long, narrow neck, and her chest and her sweet, soft cleavage. He sucks in his breath and grips the chair hard with both hands.

She looks up slantways at him, and if her mouth wasn't stuffed full of his hard dick, he'd swear she was smirking. She makes him feel used. Whether she's fucking his ass or swallowing him. Like she's got him all figured out.

But figuring it out is bullshit, she says. She tells him she'd need a whole additional lifetime just to decipher the meaning of each fuck she's had in this one.

Accept it. Don't think about why.

So he doesn't wonder why they're here, like this, at all. Or why she wanted him to wear the boots today. He just watches the tips of her hair graze the glossy leather as her head moves. He feels the pressure build in the lower part of his belly and his ass and balls. Feels the tingle in the tip of his dick every time the muscles of her throat contract around it.

He keeps his feet planted firmly on the floor and thrusts his hips forward. He ignores her knowing eyes and accepts her submissive posture, accepts his compliance, without shame. It's okay to simply live this, to simply enjoy her. Don't worry about what it means.

He comes hard. He doesn't try to give her a chance to swallow. When it spills on her chin and her chest and the white sweater, he doesn't force guilt down over the thrill in his stomach. He smiles.

She smiles back, wipes her chin and her clothes with her fingers, and sucks them clean.

"I have to run now," she says. "You'll fuck me later."

Neither request nor promise. Just a statement of fact.

Because they have to. Because they're human.

Because when they do, they're not just going through the motions.

She gives him a light, lazy, summer afternoon kind of kiss on his cheek. Her hair smells sweet and his come smells sharp, like sex, a smell like nothing else in the world.

"See ya later," he says. And then: "I love you." He wants to say it, so he does. She pauses. Her eyebrows arch a little upward, but she only smiles again. She ruffles his hair and leaves the room, and he watches her go. He loves the way her ass moves. He loves to watch her, smell her, feel her.

Love isn't the right word, but it's the only one he can find to express his—their—meaning. He looks down at his dick: sucked clean as a fucking whistle.

He shakes his head, laughs, and reaches to unlace the boots.

TO FEEL SEXY

Jordana Winters

She stared at the clock in the lower right-hand corner of her computer monitor. Her eyes were growing heavy. *4:20.* Forty minutes to go. She was fighting hard to stay awake. The paperwork in front of her ultimately required her attention but, really, she couldn't care less.

Her mind drifted to what she was going to do that night, what she was going to eat for dinner. She tried to think of anything other than her work. Her thoughts turned to Brandon—her pseudo-significant other.

Nina had been so enamored with him from the start. Their relationship wasn't a complicated one and that suited them both. They hung out, fucked, loved, and respected each other, but there was never any future or commitment talk.

He had the ability to get her cunt wet by doing nothing much at all. Oftentimes it was nothing more than a look.

Brandon wasn't the type to waste time on sweet talk. She could count on one hand how many compliments he'd thrown her way, and even then they had always been camouflaged.

"You're looking especially freaky tonight," he'd said when she had dressed in shiny black boots and a fishnet shirt, on her way to a concert. She'd had to confirm if "freaky" was a good thing. It had been.

With her past lovers, Nina had so enjoyed the showing—the dressing up in stay-ups and stockings under skirts, lacy underwear, and tight corsetlike tops.

Now, she couldn't remember how long it had been since the last time she'd put an effort into dressing up. She thought of all the clothes hanging in her closet that she hadn't worn in many months.

She wanted to feel sexy again. She *needed* to feel sexy. At this point she needed to do it for no one other than herself.

Nina was an attractive woman to be sure. Both men and women had told her so often enough. A four-day-a-week gym regime made her figure a picture of perfection. Granted, she didn't need her ego stroked anymore. Just the same it would be nice to evoke some kind of reaction from him, to hear that he found her hot, beautiful—something.

She recalled getting dressed in the morning before heading to work at her former job. At times, choosing an outfit had been an ordeal but in a pleasant way. Choosing between half a dozen pair of garters could get frustrating when she was already late, but at least she'd had the option.

Now, working in a small office with two women who took the term *casual dress* quite literally, putting a skirt on for work seemed ridiculous. Regardless, she'd woken up that morning, opened her closet doors, and opted to wear her most flattering skirt.

Brandon, the manager of a tattoo studio, was also scheduled to work today. She'd been watching the clock all day, desperate.

When five o'clock finally arrived, she was out the door without a backward glance, in her car, and on the way to the studio.

She made eye contact with Brandon through the windows as she walked up. He was on the phone, yet when she walked in, his eyes swept down her legs. She couldn't recall if he'd ever seen her in a skirt—in the summer, sure, but not in business attire, which today consisted of a tight pin-striped skirt, stockings, and heels.

Once he hung up the phone, she said, "I'm visiting," smiling coyly.

"I see that."

"I probably should have called first."

"No one else is here. I've been bored."

She walked behind the counter. "I've missed you," she purred and leaned against his chest, nuzzling in his neck, and heavily breathing in his scent.

"I like this," he said quietly.

He "liked" it. That was most likely the best she was going to get, but it was something. Clearly, she'd gotten his attention.

She felt his hand slide down her back to rest on her ass.

"Look what's underneath," she murmured, and kissed his neck.

She pulled at her skirt to show the top of her garters. His hand reached down to grab at the strap. He pulled the elastic, then let go, and it snapped pleasantly against the skin of her thigh. She leaned against the counter seductively with her skirt still hiked up around her waist. It hadn't occurred to her that someone could walk in at any time, but she watched as Brandon scribbled *back in ten minutes* on a piece of paper and taped it to the door.

"Into the back," he barked at her.

She walked to the back, with him behind her. He pushed her

through the open doorway of the piercing booth, and she turned and grabbed at his belt, loosened and undid it, then started on his fly. She reached down the front of his boxers to feel his growing hardness. Her own wetness had moistened her underwear, which now pressed pleasantly against her skin.

Hooking his thumbs through her panties and garters, he slid them down her thighs. He pushed her onto the chair, then pulled her ass forward so she was balancing on the edge. She watched as Brandon pulled his boxers and jeans down and let them fall around his knees. He grabbed at his cock and gave it a few strokes. It bobbed out ahead of him at full attention.

He sunk to his knees and buried his head between her legs. She wrapped her legs around his shoulders. He alternated between flicking her clit with his thumb and tongue while he moved his fingers deep inside her.

Nina caught sight of herself in the mirror that hung on the wall directly across from them. Her lids were half-closed, her eyes glazed over in a look of lust. She could feel her juices running down past her ass crack. She imagined she'd leave a mark on the vinyl seat.

"Your cock, please," she begged, desperate to have his fullness inside her.

"Get up," he commanded, and she jumped to her feet. He grabbed her by the shoulders, spun her around, and bent her over the chair. He was in her in one swift motion, his thickness filling her completely.

He grabbed at her shoulder with one hand and her hip with the other. He was pumping her hard from behind, quickly finding a delicious rhythm. She turned to look in the mirror. She could see his cock sliding in and out of her.

"You watching?"

She whimpered quietly as he continued pumping into her. She

felt warmth in her cunt. She was close. He knew her well enough by now to tell. He grabbed her hair, pulling her head back.

"Look at me when I fuck you," he ordered and turned her head.

That was it, all she needed. He knew just what to say. She loved when he made her look him in the eye. She glared at him until she came. He kept pumping, warmth vibrating and coursing through her cunt.

His hand tightened harder around the back of her neck and her waist. Gasping, he emptied himself in her, then pulled out.

"Here," he said and handed her a roll of paper towel, then leaned against the wall.

She wiped her thighs clean and pulled up her panties and garters. She leaned forward and kissed him quickly as he pulled on his boxers and pants.

Five minutes later, she was sitting out front with him, listening to him recount the stories of his day. She was sticky between her legs, and somewhat tousled all over, but still feeling very sexy.

ON ISLAND TIME

Kristina Wright

Hannah sat across from Kyle, enjoying a decadent dinner at their island resort's restaurant as waves lapped at the beach and seagulls screeched overhead. She closed her eyes and sighed contentedly. St. Thomas was perfect; every detail was so romantic and decadent.

"You look like a satisfied woman," Kyle observed.

She opened her eyes and smiled. "Mmm, in some ways. In other ways, I'm far from satisfied."

She lowered her eyes, enjoying playing the tease—for now. She moaned softly as she took another bite of her meal, savoring the delicate combination of spices and mango glaze that complemented the fresh catch of the day. "Stop that," Kyle chastised. "You've already got me hard as a rock and all you're doing is eating dinner."

Hannah stared deeply into his eyes and slowly licked her lips. "Maybe I should skip dessert and nibble on you, hmm?"

Kyle's expression was priceless. He didn't get a chance

to respond to her suggestion, however, because the waiter approached at that moment. He waited until the man was out of earshot to say, "You're a naughty tease and I would love to take you up on that offer, but we have our massage appointment after dinner, remember?"

"Oh, I remember," she said, shifting in her chair. The hem of her purple dress fluttered up and the warm ocean breeze caressed her bare thighs. "I can't wait."

They finished their dinner, teasing and flirting with each other like two strangers who couldn't wait to get into bed. The sexual tension hung heavy in the air, and Hannah was reminded of the fact she wasn't wearing underwear every time Kyle said something that made her squirm. She had a brief moment of apprehension that she might actually leave a wet spot on the back of her dress, but she pushed it aside. She was enjoying this long, slow seduction scene too much to worry about anything. As Kyle kept reminding her, they were on island time now. All that mattered was pleasure.

Kyle signed the bill and guided her down the hibiscus-lined walkway to the spa. An iguana scurried across the flag-stone path in front of them, and Hannah let out a soft shriek as it disappeared into the shrubbery with a flutter of leaves. Kyle chuckled, his hand warm and strong against the small of her back. She found herself pressing against him, wanting to be as close to him as she could possibly be. As if sensing her need, Kyle wrapped his arms around her from behind, cupping and kneading her breasts through the thin fabric of her dress.

She sighed and whimpered softly as her nipples stiffened under his touch. "Maybe we should skip the massages and go back to our room."

"No, you've been looking forward to this," Kyle said, his

voice rough with lust. "I'll take care of you when we get back to the room."

"Promise?"

He tweaked her hard nipples through her dress. "Oh, I promise."

A young blonde woman greeted them at the spa and led them into the couples' massage room. They were instructed to undress and stretch out beneath the sheets on the tables. As soon as the door closed, Kyle reached for Hannah. She giggled and pulled away.

"No, no. You told me I had to wait, now you have to wait!" She slipped out of her dress and stood naked in front of him with her hands on her hips. "See what you're missing?"

Kyle stared at her, his gaze taking in every inch of her naked body before settling on the bare mound of her pussy. "Want to see what you're missing?"

"Let me," she whispered.

She reached for his belt and undid his pants, grazing his sizeable erection with the back of her hand. She pushed his pants down over his hips, freeing his cock. She moaned softly and sank to her knees in front of him. Before he could protest, she wrapped her lips around the head of his cock and began sucking him.

"Oh, babe." He stroked her hair softly. "Your mouth feels so good on me."

She wrapped her hand around his rigid shaft and took him deeper into her mouth. He rewarded her with a low moan that grew louder when she slipped her saliva-wet fingers between his thighs and cupped his heavy balls. He shifted his weight, spreading his legs slightly. "I'm going to explode if you don't stop," he warned.

She didn't want to stop. She wanted to make him come... hard. He was close, she could feel it in the way his cock throbbed in her mouth. She swirled her tongue around the head while she stroked his shaft. He twisted his fingers in her hair and moaned deeply. Just a few more moments and he would come for her.

"Oh, baby, suck me," he murmured. "I'm going to come."

She gripped his ass with one hand, pulling him deeper into her mouth. He came with a deep, guttural groan, his cock twitching and swelling in her mouth. Hot semen splashed the back of her throat and she swallowed everything he gave her, her whimpers muffled by his cock.

She was so lost in the taste and feel of him, she didn't realize someone was knocking on the door until Kyle pulled free of her sucking mouth.

"One minute," Kyle said, sounding out of breath as he helped Hannah to her feet. "Bad girl. Wait until I get you back to the room."

"I can't wait." She slid a finger between the lips of her pussy and showed him the wetness glistening there. "I need to get fucked."

Kyle wrapped his fingers around her wrist and pulled her hand to his mouth. He sucked her juices off her finger. "Oh, you will, baby. You will."

They quickly arranged themselves under the soft, white sheets on the massage tables just as the door opened and the two masseuses came in. Hannah licked her lips and winked at Kyle before giving herself over to the talented hands of her masseuse. Naughty thoughts ran through her mind as her body was oiled and massaged with steady, soothing strokes. She sighed and moaned softly, every touch of the masseuse's smooth hands conjuring up images of Kyle's hands on her body, his cock in her mouth.

"Does that feel good?" the woman asked softly, as she worked warm oil into the muscles of Hannah's shoulders.

"Mmm, yes."

An hour later, Hannah was both relaxed and aroused and more than ready to take Kyle back to their room. Her skin smelled sweetly of almonds and was sensitive to the touch. Wet heat pooled between her thighs, making her even more aware she wasn't wearing panties under her dress.

"Ready to go back to the room?"

She tucked her arm into his as they walked out into the balmy night air and sighed. "You have no idea how ready I am." Hannah had never needed to get fucked more than she did right that moment. Her entire body throbbed with the need to be touched and filled. The almond massage oil that scented her skin only served as an additional aphrodisiac, tantalizing her imagination with thoughts of her soft, oiled body naked and entwined with Kyle's.

They walked hand in hand down the beach to their ocean-front room, pausing every dozen steps or so to kiss and touch each other. It was romantic and maddening at the same time. She wanted him so badly, but she didn't want to rush a single moment of this night. Island time, she reminded herself. They had all night.

The beach was empty except for a couple sitting in the sand near the ocean's edge. They were so lost in each other they didn't notice Kyle and Hannah walking by, or when Hannah's dress fluttered up and bared her ass. Kyle took the opportunity to give her a sharp smack before she managed to pull the dress back down.

She gasped, more in surprise than pain. The sting of the slap faded immediately to a dull throb that seemed concentrated between her legs. "Oh! I'll get you for that," she called over her shoulder as she ran the last few steps to their room. Kyle caught up to her and let her into the room, following her inside.

The full moon illuminated the room with soft, shimmering light, and her body throbbed in anticipation as she pushed him down on the king-sized bed and sprawled across him. They kissed like teenagers, tongues exploring open mouths, hands groping over clothing in the near darkness. Hannah's dress rode up to her waist and she felt Kyle's hands roaming over her bottom, rubbing and squeezing until all she wanted was his fingers inside her. She wasn't quite ready to let him off the hook for smacking her, though.

"I want you naked," she said. She moved away and turned on the lamp beside the bed. "I want to see you."

Kyle wasted no time in getting undressed, his erection just as hard and huge as it had been in the spa.

"I see you've recovered from that blow job," she teased.

He grinned. "You have that effect on me."

She made an appreciative sound low in her throat as he adjusted himself, but she didn't touch him. She felt so hot and nasty, she wanted to make this a night they would both remember for a long, long time.

"Sit in the chair," she said, gesturing to the desk by the window. "But turn it around so it faces the bed."

"Why?"

"Just do it. I promise you won't be disappointed."

He moved the chair into place and sat down, watching her with a bemused expression as she went to the bureau. She pulled out a few things and tucked them under the edge of the bedspread so he wouldn't see, then she crossed the room to where he sat.

"Put your hands behind your back."

He stared at her as he silently obeyed, his erection thick and heavy against his thigh. "What are you going to do to me?"

She bound his hands to the back of the chair with his belt. When she was satisfied that he couldn't free himself, she sat on the edge of the bed. "Nothing. You're just going to watch."

He groaned. "Tease."

She pulled her vibrator from under the spread and showed it to him. "You have no idea."

She slid the vibrator under the hem of her dress and turned it on low speed. She gasped the moment she touched the tip of the cool, vibrating plastic to her engorged clitoris. Kyle stared between her legs as if he could see what she was doing, but her dress hid all the action. She closed her eyes as she massaged her clit with the vibrator, whimpering softly. Over and over, she stroked her clit with the vibrator, bringing herself close to orgasm. When she knew she couldn't take much more of her own teasing, she spread her legs wider and slid the tip of the vibrator into her wet pussy.

"Show me what you're doing," Kyle whispered.

She was too far gone to deny him. With her free hand, she flipped up the hem of her dress, showing him the vibrator sliding into her smooth, bare pussy. "Do you like that?" she asked.

He swallowed hard and nodded. "You are so hot. I want to be inside you."

She wanted him inside her, too. The vibrator felt good, but it wasn't enough, she wanted more. So much more.

"Not yet, baby," she whispered. "We're on island time, remember?"

"Don't tease me. I need you."

She pushed the vibrator inside her as far as it would go, feeling the vibrations throbbing through her body. "That's where I want you," she said. "Deep inside me."

His only response was a long, low moan.

She pulled the vibrator out of her pussy and turned it off. Her body still felt like it was vibrating as she stood on shaky legs and untied him. He was on her in a moment, pushing her back down on the edge of the bed, and kneeling on the floor between her legs. Her eyes fluttered closed and she lay back as he slid his fingers into her wetness. His warm skin felt so much better than hard plastic. She pulled the top of her dress down and squeezed and fondled her breasts, the combination of sensations driving her mad with need.

"Do you like that, baby?"

"Oh, yes," she whispered. "I want more."

"I'll give you anything you want."

She loved the sounds of her wet pussy being fucked by his fingers. His touch felt so good, but she wanted more. She wanted to be filled.

"More," she whispered again.

"I already have three fingers inside you," he said, fucking her with steady thrusts. "You want another finger?"

"Yes," she breathed softly. "Please."

It took her body a moment to adjust to accomodating four fingers, but soon her wetness lubricated his fingers and allowed him to glide inside her. She braced her feet on the edge of the bed, knees up and spread open to his gaze and his touch.

"Is that good, baby?"

"Mmm…so good." Her throat was so dry she could barely hear her own voice.

"Your bare pussy is so sexy," Kyle murmured. "I love fucking you like this."

She could barely seem to catch her breath. It was too much, it was just enough. She couldn't tell if she was going to laugh or cry at the feeling of his fingers stretching her pussy, she only knew she loved the sensation. She gasped and whimpered, thrashing on the bed as he worked his fingers inside her. She could feel her orgasm building and she reached for it, every muscle in her body taut with arousal.

"Come for me, baby," Kyle said, his voice rough with lust. "Come on my fingers. Come for me so I can fuck you."

She moaned low in her throat as her pussy contracted around his hand. "Now, now," she gasped, the words barely coherent. "I'm coming!"

Kyle pinned her to the bed with his shoulder against her thigh, his fingers thrusting inside her. Her orgasm crashed over her, taking her breath away. It went on and on in endless waves of sensation and emotion that brought tears to her eyes as she screamed and panted. She clutched at Kyle, touching whatever part of him she could reach before gripping his wrist where it touched her body.

"Fuck me, fuck me," she said, giving his wrist a gentle tug. She felt a little gush of liquid as he pulled his fingers free of her pussy. "I want to feel your cock inside me."

"Are you sure you want more?"

"Oh, yes," she breathed. "I want more."

His hands were gentle on her body as he took off her dress and rolled her over. She got on her hands and knees, her pussy still throbbing from her orgasm. Kyle stood and stroked her hips and ass. She whimpered low in her throat, nearly out of her mind with desire.

"I want you inside me," she said again.

Kyle placed the tip of his cock at her opening and slowly slid inside her, inch by excruciating inch. "Is that what you want, baby?"

She whimpered in response.

As if he had reached his breaking point, Kyle gripped her hips and pulled her firmly back on his cock. Deep inside her now, he gave her what she had wanted since dinner. She moved on his cock as he fucked her with slow, steady strokes. She felt so wet and swollen as her body took the full length of his cock.

"You feel so good," he whispered.

He pulled back until only the head of his cock was nestled between the lips of her pussy before sliding into her once again. He made love to her slowly, almost gently, and she sensed the control it took for him not to fuck her hard. He was doing it for her, to make her feel good, but she wanted him to lose control the way she had.

"That's it, fuck me," she encouraged. "I want it. Fuck me hard."

Her words seemed to drive him over the edge. He gripped her hips tighter and fucked her roughly. Her pussy felt swollen and bruised, but his cock felt so good she didn't care. She braced her elbows on the bed, raising her ass to him as he drove himself into her.

His breathing changed and she knew he was going to come. She pushed back against him as hard as he was thrusting into her, giving as good as she was getting.

"Yes, baby, yes," she gasped.

He moaned as he came, clinging to her damp body as his cock throbbed inside her. She dropped to the bed and he collapsed on top of her, both of them breathing hard.

"That was incredible." He moved off her, brushing her hair out of her face. "I love you so much."

"I love you, too." She giggled softly. "And I love being on island time."

VIEW OF A ROOM

Jason McFadden

As I walked from the driveway toward our steep front steps, I heard a rapping noise. My head was down, thoughts of work still swimming through my mind. But there it was again: *Tap, tap, tap.*

When I looked up, I saw Olivia waiting for me. Now that she'd gotten my attention, she stood totally still in our floor-to-ceiling picture window, staring down at me with a sexy smile on her beautiful face. This wouldn't have been an entirely unusual pastime for my lovely wife—our view is almost as inexplicably gorgeous as Olivia herself, a vast panorama of a silver sand beach, the immense Golden Gate Bridge, and the deep-blue waters of the San Francisco Bay. Olivia often spends time admiring this vision at the end of her day, claiming that there's no better way to unwind from the pressures of work.

At least, *almost* no better way.

However, tonight was different. Because tonight Olivia was entirely naked, her long strawberry-blonde hair spilling over her shoulders, the succulent curves of her hourglass figure totally open to me—and to any other person who happened to be passing by. A concept which made me hard on the spot.

Quickly, I raced up the front stairs and into the house, all thoughts of business evaporating like morning fog over the water. I couldn't get indoors fast enough. But once I opened the front door, I hesitated, gazing in silent awe at Olivia's naked form as a surge of excitement flared through me. Every light in the room was on, and lit crimson candles gleamed on the mantle and on the coffee table. The candlelight created a warm, golden glow, while the rest of the lights made sure that everything in the room was visible from the outside. Olivia had obviously planned this encounter down to the minutest detail.

"Hey, Cord," she grinned, turning to watch me enter. Her pale skin was luminous in the light, her violet eyes flashing at me. I could tell that she was smiling at the fact that she'd rendered me speechless by her bold behavior. "Aren't you going to come all of the way inside?" she teased.

Almost in a daze, I closed the door behind me and then walked slowly forward.

Olivia stood half-turned toward me, one hand on the pane of glass, a come-hither smile on her glossy scarlet-slicked lips. "Take off your clothes, Cord," she purred, causing my heart to start racing even faster. Her husky voice held a note of humor in it, but the command was intensely demanding, nevertheless. I love when Olivia takes charge of our X-rated encounters. She possesses one of the most delightfully dirty minds I've had the pleasure to know, constantly choreographing passionate plans for the two of us. Still, from the sultry way she stood before me, naked except for a pair of killer open-toed high-heeled sandals, I thought I had an idea of exactly what tonight's plan might be. Although we engage in many different naughty games together, our favorite erotic activity by far is to make love where people can see us—and the very best place to be seen is right in our window.

We live in the exclusive Marina District of San Francisco, and although our townhouse is fairly modest in comparison to some of the more luxurious homes around us—the ones built to look like Italian villas, or the bows of yachts, or fairytale castles—just like the other locations to our left and right, our more humble abode still boasts a generous picture window in the living room. Floor to ceiling, the window takes up the entire front wall of the living room. And Olivia was holding court dead in the center.

The Marina is a famous destination for travelers. Day and night, tourists drive slowly down our winding street, taking in the picture postcard view of the bridge and the bay on the water side and the 1920s-style opulent architecture on the street side. Some of our neighbors find the constant attention intrusive, but Olivia and I don't mind. In fact, we look forward to the multitudes of people passing by our windows—all those strangers staring, their eyes on us.

"Come on, Cord, get your sexy ass over here—"

At Olivia's instruction, I immediately moved forward, stripping off my clothes as I walked—unable to undress myself fast enough. I wanted to be naked. *Now.* First off came my black leather jacket, then my crisp olive green button-down shirt and the white T-shirt beneath. My fingers fumbled in their hurry to undo my favorite old brown belt, and I had to stop for a moment to kick off my engineer boots before finally getting rid of my jeans. I was at her side by this time, down now to my sapphire-striped boxer-briefs, unable to keep my hands off my stunning wife for another second. My cock would have reached her first, the way it was standing at full attention, had it not still been trapped within the confines of my undershorts.

"You're late," she smiled at me. She spoke as if I'd held her up for a planned event—an evening at the opera, perhaps, or a night on the town, which wasn't the case at all. I was simply home later than usual because traffic had been disastrous this evening. But I understood precisely what her little comment meant. She'd been waiting for me, naked, her pussy growing wetter with each passing minute and each passing car. And now as I touched her, I imagined all of the other people out there who might have seen her while she stood in our second-floor window, on the lookout for me.

My hands gripped her slim waist, forcefully pulling her against me, letting her feel how turned on I'd become at the thought. I was like steel, ready for her, set to spread her out against the chilly plate glass window and have my way with her. But Olivia had other ideas. First, she let her hand wander down between us, carefully caressing my hard-on through my boxers, before her playful fingers reached all the way down to gently cup my balls.

"Oh, god," I sighed, loving her touch, as always. Olivia responded by gripping on to my rod through the thin fabric, giving me a firm tug, and I swallowed hard, wanting to explode—wanting to sprint for the finish line. But that's not the way Olivia plays. She likes to take things slowly, stretch things out. Yet that doesn't mean she torments me. With grace, she slid her hand into the slit of the shorts, then continued to jack her fist on my shaft as I bent my head down to hers for our first kiss of the evening.

Her hot mouth pressed to mine, chastely at first, and then our tongues met. I felt the tiny silver curl of her tongue ring, lost myself momentarily in the warmth of her breasts against my bare chest. Kissing Olivia made my cock throb even harder in the luscious embrace of her fist. But then she pulled away from me, giving me a look from under her thick, dark lashes, letting me know with her deep blue-purple eyes alone exactly what she wanted from me.

I dipped my head again, now kissing along the elegant under curve of her long neck before slowly licking along the delicate lines of her collarbone. As I kissed her, she took my hands in hers and placed them on her body, exactly where she wanted them, cradling the curves of her breathtaking derriere.

"Touch me," she whispered. "Touch me *everywhere*, Cord—"

I obeyed her request immediately, palming the bewitching apples of her asscheeks before spreading them slightly as I kissed and licked my way down her body. I imagined drivers seeing the sweet reveal of Olivia's rear view, and I took a moment to peek over her shoulder, to see if I was right.

"Are there people out there?" she murmured, needing to know. "Are they watching—?"

Looking outside, I saw a couple strolling hand in hand along the sand, lost in the moonlit evening. A car passed by, and then another, and then a motorcyclist headed in our direction. I saw his eyes widen as he caught sight of my lovely lady's naked figure, and he craned his head to catch one last look before rounding the corner. When he gunned his engine and turned around for a second look, his motion caught the strolling couple's attention. And when they turned to see what was going on, they saw Olivia.

As I whispered to Olivia that yes, people were watching, she sighed and slipped her hips forward and back, first pressing hard into me, and then back into the cool glass of the window, rocking her hips in constant motion. Nothing turns Olivia on more than being seen.

I kissed her more fiercely, now moving my hands along the length of her body, whispering in between kisses that the couple was still watching. That they could see everything. That they wanted to see more.

"How do you know?" she whispered.

"I just know."

Her skin was silky under my touch and it grew warmer still as I continued to stroke her like a kitty, fondling her hips with the flat of my hands, then bending on my knees as I slid my hands down her legs, all the way to the tips of her cherry red toenails peeking out of her open-toed sandals.

"Tell me, Cord," she begged. "Are they still there?"

"Yeah, baby," I assured her. "They're watching me kiss you. I'll bet the lady wishes her man would treat her the same way."

Olivia sighed in agreement, and when I glanced up at her, I saw that she had closed her eyes and tilted her head back, clearly basking in the feeling of my fingertips running all over her body. The candlelight cast dreamy shadows over us both, but what turned me on even more was the way headlights from outside slid over our figures before dancing across the far wall. This was just one more reminder that there were people out there—San Francisco is a bustling city—and undoubtedly those people could see us.

For several moments, I thought of this sexy scenario while teasing my tongue back up the insides of Olivia's legs, my fingers still stroking over the flat of her belly, the curves of her body.

As creative director for a local art-house magazine, Olivia has the ability to be avant-garde. There's no need for her to try to be a dress-for-success type, and she gives in to her artistic yearnings. Accompanying her pierced tongue, she also sports several colorful tattoos adorning her perfect body. Now I traced the one on her right hip with the tip of my tongue before changing positions to press my lips to the butterfly resting on her inner thigh. From here, I could breathe in deeply to catch the heady scent of

Olivia's arousal. She was so turned on, and her visible excitement thrilled me even more. I knew that she'd been waiting for me in the window, but I wondered how long she'd stood there. Had she touched herself while imagining me touching her, waiting for me to finally arrive home to make her fantasies come true?

I focused my attention on the delicious treat of dining on my pretty wife's pussy.

Oh, lord, she was sweet. My tongue tasted the decadent drops of her delicious wetness and then probed forward, searching for more. From our years of experience together, I know just how to touch her, understand exactly the type of treatment she craves, and now I made tantalizing rings around her clit before sucking it into my mouth. Olivia moaned and dug her fingernails firmly into my shoulders as once again I thought about what we must look like to any passing viewers: Olivia's sensational figure seen from behind is enough to make any man weak in the legs. She has a crimson-hued cherry tattoo on her left cheek and a fuchsia rose vine climbing from ankle to midthigh. I didn't think any tourists would be able to see those intricate details so clearly, but I knew they'd be able to see Olivia's ripe, round ass, and me on my knees in front of her—it would be clear to anyone that I was drinking from her, dining from her.

The dizzy motion of traveling headlights swept over the far wall of our apartment again and again, and a matching shudder ran through Olivia every time. I could tell that she was thinking exactly what I was, imagining those drivers watching her, those tourists getting more than they bargained for as they cruised through our lovely city by the bay.

My tongue made a devious, spiraling route around Olivia's clit, keeping her off balance, so that she never knew exactly when I would brush against that pulsing little button directly, giving her the sensation she so desperately craved. Would I tease her mercilessly, until she begged me to touch her exactly how she wished? Or would I take pity, rapping my tongue against her clit in perfect rhythm, sending her reeling with palpitations of pleasure? She didn't have a clue, which is exactly what I wanted.

In spite of my own building excitement, I took my time treating her in the manner she deserved, feeling her desperation grow stronger as she gripped on to my shoulders harder still, pushing her hips forward to further attempt to seal her pussy to my mouth. I savored the way her creamy juices spread to my lips, coating my face as I turned my head gently back and forth, letting my short dark hair tickle her inner thighs so that she squealed with pleasure. She was so ready, so hungry, that finally I found I could deny her no longer. With force, I ground my mouth harder against her, taking her where she needed to go.

Or close. So close.

"Are they still watching?" she murmured.

I peered through the V of her legs, looking at the couple out there on the sand, standing mesmerized as they stared into our window.

"Yes," I told her. "They're watching. They can see you."

Olivia's orgasm stretched out, the contractions shaking her whole body, and she moaned, rocking her hips back and forth even more quickly, gleaning every last bit of pleasure from the tip of my tongue. Her normally pale skin was flushed, and her pussy was so wet that the juices had dampened her inner thighs. But that wasn't enough for my ravenous lover.

"Oh, god," Olivia whimpered, the pleasure winging through her. "Oh, god—" Yet as soon as she caught her breath, Olivia grabbed my hand and pulled me, taking me upstairs after her. I knew precisely where we were headed—to the balcony off of our bedroom. She'd had her time in the picture window.

Now, she wanted to fuck outside.

* * *

From the way Olivia hurried to the railing on our balcony, I could tell that she wanted immediate satisfaction. Even though she'd only just climaxed moments before, it was as if that action had been merely the appetizer of the evening's erotic events, and now she was ready and raring for the main course. When I met her at the railing, she was instantly on me, pushing recklessly with her fingers on the waistband of my striped boxers, hurrying to get me entirely undressed so that I would match her nakedness. She was going to face forward now, to face her audience head on. I saw that the couple had found a seat on the green wooden bench across the street. They were still staring at us, their arms around each other to stay warm, watching us as if we were a show put on for their pleasure alone—when really, they were the ones giving us the pleasure that we so deeply desired.

"Fuck me," Olivia demanded, facing forward now, her palms on the iron railing, offering me her ever-delightful rear view. "Fuck me hard, Cord!"

I didn't need any further instruction. My cock had been at full-mast since I'd first looked up and caught her waiting for me in the nude. Now, as the cool night breeze swept over us both, I pressed my body to hers, letting her feel precisely how hard I was. Olivia moaned softly, sweetly, and pressed back against me, demanding without words, craving the type of act that I knew would make her feel complete.

Although I always do enjoy forcing her to wait, knowing that anticipation is one of the world's most decadent aphrodisiacs, I didn't have the heart for it now. Not with people watching. Not with us so truly on display. Our time in the picture window was all the foreplay I could handle. Right now, I had to be inside of her, had to feel her wetness envelop me, her inner muscles welcome me.

Gently, I split apart her cheeks with my hands as I slid inside of her pussy. Then I looked down, reveling in the view of my cock disappearing to the hilt within her. I loved that vision almost as much as the view in front of us: the bridge, the boats, the hulking island of Alcatraz. I stared down, watching my cock thrust inside of her, then emerge again, glistening with her most private wetness. But then, because I am as much of an exhibitionist as my daring wife, I found myself drawn to gaze out beyond the balcony, seeing exactly what Olivia was seeing—the million-dollar view before us. The bay was decorated with the ghostly white sails of the passing sailboats, the sulfur-yellow lights outlining the bridge, the row of swaying palm trees—but more important to our own personal fetish—that quiet duo out there in the dark.

They were catching their own million-dollar view, seeing my stunning Olivia facing forward, her body a dream, her face a vision of the purest form of ecstasy. Even from behind, I could easily imagine the expression of rapture on her face: her dark violet eyes open, her stunning bee-stung lips parted.

I gripped her thick rope of hair as I fucked her, holding her steady by her long, red-blonde mane, my fist lost in her hair, tightening my hold with each thrust. She sighed and bucked against me, and I slammed in with greater force, the hardest that I'd been all night, driving my cock inside her to the very hilt, relishing the crisp chill of the night air as together we made our own heat.

The power of our passion matched the crash of the waves on the sand, surpassed the rhythm of the traffic on the Golden Gate Bridge. What were all those people thinking as they traveled along the famous span? If they looked out of the safety of their cars and saw us, would they become as erotically intoxicated as we were? Would they possibly be inspired to create their own Tantric tableau?

Again and again I slammed against her, and then reached one hand in front of her waist and stroked her still-throbbing clit. Olivia mewed hungrily as I played her, patting her clit in tandem with the thrusts of my rock-hard cock inside of her. I could tell she was reaching her limits from the way that she began to breathe, almost panting, faster and faster. And then I was sprinting along with her, feeling the impending orgasm build within me. Pleasure came for us both then as we reached the point of our climax together, staring out at the city, lost in our own explicit embrace.

Olivia sighed and leaned back against me, making sure that I was still locked inside of her, kept prisoner within her. I looked down at her, saw the mesmerizing glow of her white skin, the vibrant colors of her tattoos, the spill of her hair now that I'd let it free from my grip.

In silence, the couple across the way stood and moved on down the path, heading to their own adventures, perhaps in a window or on a balcony of their own.

As Olivia and I parted and headed back inside, I thought of how lucky we are to live here. Some of our neighbors complain about the constant crush of tourists on our roads, but Olivia and I don't mind—it's the price you pay for million-dollar views. Tonight, though, I think the best view in San Francisco was of us.

DATE AT SOUTH STATION

Xavier Acton

South Station was not in the best part of town, which is why it was so freakin' weird that Shannon wanted to be picked up there. "I've got a meeting there," Shannon had told him. "My car's in the shop."

"What the hell kind of meeting do you have at South Station?" he asked.

She'd gotten a weird pleased enigmatic look on her face, and said: "Actually, it's more of a date." When he looked confused, she said, "Don't ask questions you don't want to know the answer to, hon."

"Hon?"

She rolled her eyes.

"And you're taking the underground there? I don't think that's very safe."

"I'll cab it from the office. Oh, and I'm going to leave my raincoat in your trunk."

"Your raincoat? What the fuck?"

"In case it's cold when you pick me up."

"It's been over a hundred."

"Don't ask questions, darling. It doesn't become you."

So here Keith was at eight on a Friday, cruising down West Blake between the South Station entrance and a parking garage with barred gates and armed guards. He was more than a little nervous even just driving here in the new Porsche; he kind of felt like he was advertising for a carjacking. As a matter of fact, he thought that was what was happening when suddenly a whore in a tight skirt and tube top stepped out in front of him. Traffic was slow and he was only going about fifteen miles an hour, so he slammed on the brakes as she came toward the car. He panicked: he'd read about this; she distracts him while some guy comes up—wait, was that Shannon? She came up to the driver's side window and bent down low, her perfect round apple-tits hanging out of the tiny tube top.

"Shannon?" he asked.

"Want a date, hon?" she asked him. Her hair was bobbed and freshly bleached—or she was wearing a wig. The red tube top was practically see-through, and the skirt was far from decent. She had a black dog collar around her pale throat. He couldn't be sure, but she looked nothing like Shannon—except that she did. "Ooh, this is a nice car, is this yours? Take me for a ride!" She said "ride" with a salacious dragging out of all its syllables—all eight of them, the way she said it.

"Shannon, is that you?"

"Sure," she said. "You can call me 'Shannon' if you like." She shimmied her body and flashed her perfect tits at him. "I'll be anyone you like."

Keith desperately looked around for cops or drug dealers. "Get in the car!" he snapped.

"Don't have to ask me twice," said Shannon, opening the

door of the Porsche and slipping into the deep bucket seat. Her legs splayed and her skirt climbed up; even through the shock and dismay, Keith had to admit her legs looked damn good in that short skirt and those impossibly high heels.

A lowrider behind him honked. He hit the gas before Shannon even closed the door, and she tittered. "Can't wait, can you, baby? Don't worry, I won't make you."

"Have you gone fucking insane?" he asked as he steered through the heavy traffic and looked for a place to turn off and cut back to the freeway. "Are you totally crazy?"

She got an innocent look on her face.

"Crazy for you, baby," she said. "Your car turns me on. You can't expect a girl to let a car like this just drive by, can you?" She curled up in the seat without putting on her seat belt, leaning close to him and caressing the side of his face with the long fake fingernails of her left hand—those, too, were new. "Can you blame a girl for wanting to meet a nice guy like you and have some fun?" He hadn't noticed her other hand creeping toward him, and as she said "fun" she stuck her hand in his crotch. He yelped softly and swerved a bit.

"Could you put on your seat belt?" he asked hoarsely.

"Uh-uh," said Shannon, caressing his crotch through his dress pants. His cock began to stiffen. She made a pleased, soft sighing noise. "Not until you tell me how bad you want me, baby." She leaned close and drew her tongue in a circle around his ear. "It's fifty dollars to get my sweet mouth on your big fucking cock, hon, and a hundred if you want to go all the way."

Keith breathed hard. His cock was getting very hard, and in between strokes, Shannon would play with his belt buckle.

"A hundred bucks?"

The beam of a streetlight crossed her face, and Keith realized suddenly why she'd looked so strangely different—her normally brown eyes were bright blue; she was wearing new contacts. With the blonde hair, she looked like a completely different person; the fact that he'd recognized her at all was a testament to that perfectly unmistakable button nose of hers and how many hours he'd spent looking at her body, which was so completely exposed in the slutty little outfit.

"Uh-huh," she said. "A hundred bucks to fuck me. If that's too rich for your blood, hon," she smiled, "I think you'll love what my mouth will do on a hard cock."

He couldn't decide if he was titillated or freaked out, and he wasn't sure he wanted to play along—but fuck, she looked good in that outfit...

"Eighty," he growled.

She breathed warmly on his ear and tickled his earlobe with her tongue. "Nope. A hundred, hon. But you want to hear the good news?"

"What?" he snapped.

"I'm feeling good and horny, baby. If you want, for an extra hundred you can put it in my *ass*."

Keith swallowed.

"Your ass?"

Shannon cooed in his ear. "That's right, baby. My tight... little...back...door, hon. Let's you and me go somewhere, baby. You want to go somewhere with me?"

She was using a weird little whore voice—an old drama major's approximation of Marilyn Monroe in *Some Like It Hot* crossed with Lesley Ann Warren in *Victor/Victoria*, both of which they'd watched on their recently negotiated Chick Flick night after he had vetoed *Terms of Endearment*. He decided that even if he played along, he would refrain from countering with Arnold in *T2* from their Dude Flick night.

"Come on, baby," she sighed. "I saw how your eyes lit up.

You want to fuck my pretty ass? It's real tight. Come on, hon, take me somewhere and I'll make you feel real good."

There was a break in the traffic, and Keith took a hard right down a decrepit residential street, wincing as the Porsche hit potholes. He hit West Ellery on the far side and turned left to head up over the hill and back home. Shannon caressed his crotch the whole time, getting his cock good and hard; he had to fight to concentrate.

"Would you please put your seat belt on?"

"That depends," purred Shannon. "Are we going far?"

Her grip tightened on his cock. Keith took a quick breath. Then he spotted it: Ellery Street Motel, a run-down rattrap festering on a street corner in the middle of a big open lot.

"Right here," he said, and pulled into the parking lot, the Porsche bouncing smoothly over speed bumps.

Shannon looked impressed—more impressed than a whore would have been. She said, "I need the money first," and Keith panicked.

"I can put the room on my card," he said, lamely.

She shook her head. "I'm cash only, baby."

"I only have twenty dollars," he said.

She looked disgusted. "I've heard that before!"

She inclined her head toward the opposite corner of the intersection where there was a sleazy liquor store with a big sign that said ATM.

Shannon leaned close and almost kissed him—but not quite.

"I promise, baby," she said. "You'll *never* get better pussy."

Keith got out of the Porsche. It chirped as he locked it.

The clerk at the motel had no illusions about what was happening—or thought he didn't. But he didn't make an issue of it. Keith left Shannon with the key and walked across the street to the liquor store. The ATM had a hundred dollar limit, and after panicking and feeling his hard cock throbbing in his pants, he asked the store clerk for directions to the next closest store with an ATM. It was two blocks away, and there were two stores across the street from each other, so he hit them both. Aren't you supposed to tip whores? Keith wasn't sure, but he figured better safe than sorry. Since he got enough cash, he also picked up three little packets of lube from the display outside the bulletproof glass at the third store's register.

The whole expedition took him thirty minutes, and the sun was all the way down by the time he returned. He felt his heart pounding, and he half expected to be mugged.

He found Shannon stripped naked on the bed. Well, naked except for her high heels and the dog collar. She had her legs spread and he could see that she'd trimmed her pubic hair to a tiny little landing strip; the rest of her was shaved. As she stretched out on the bed she worked her tits with one hand and caressed her sex with the other. From the ease with which her fingers were moving, it was obvious she was good and wet. Her lips were pursed slightly and as he came in the door, they hung slightly open, letting her tongue ease out as if to beckon him.

Even the stale scent of the room and the garish polyester Shannon was spread on couldn't compete with that. He'd lost his hard-on during the walk, but he got it right back, before he even had his pants open.

"Money first," she said in a smoky voice. "Put it on the table, hon." She never stopped rubbing her puss or rhythmically pinching her nipple.

He took out two sheaves of money and laid them out on the nightstand, clawing at his shirt and pants as he did. He put down the lube, too. Shannon paused in her self-caresses and crawled across the big bed and picked up the money and counted it. She also fondled the lube.

She got a wicked look in her eye. "Well," she said. "I guess you want it around the world."

"What's that?"

"You get to know all three of me," she giggled, displaying the three hundred dollars he'd gotten out of the ATMs.

She put the money back down and got on her knees, finishing the job of undoing Keith's pants. She took out his cock and caressed it with just the tip of her tongue, running it from base to head and swirling it around. She made an audible gulping sound as she took it in her mouth and pushed his cockhead to the back of her throat. He let out a moan as she took him down without pausing.

She began working her way up and down on his cock. She bobbed up and down, caressing her pussy as she did; he undressed while she sucked him, slipping off his shirt and under-shirt and letting his pants fall to his ankles. She worked on his jockey shorts and by the time he managed to kick his shoes off, his hands were running through her hair—fuck a duck, it wasn't a wig, she'd really bleached it, and gotten a new cut and everything.

He was close enough to start breathing hard, afraid she was going to make him cum but not wanting her to stop. He couldn't bring himself to push her away; mostly he just wanted to stand there and let himself go in her hungrily sucking mouth.

Shannon knew he was going to cum, too; she looked up at him with her big blue eyes and worked his shaft with her hand as she went up and down on him. Of course she knew, he realized. She was a prostitute; she had practical considerations. He realized she was trying to get him off with the minimum investment of her time—she had the money, now it was time to get him finished and out the fucking door before he wasted any more of her precious time. Damn, Shannon was good at this game.

Well, damned if he wasn't going to get what he'd paid for. If he didn't, he was pretty sure his little whore would never forgive him.

He took hold of her hair and pulled her off of him gently.

"Let's fuck," he said, adding in an unconvinced voice: "I paid for you, now I'm going to...let's fuck." He'd lost momentum halfway through, but she got the picture.

Shannon had left his cock colored pink with lipstick. She crawled back across the bed and spread for him.

"Come on, hon," she sighed. "Fuck me. Fuck your little whore."

Keith was on her in an instant. He went to kiss her and found her turning her head; whores didn't kiss, he remembered, and that only made his cock harder. She caressed him with her slender fingers as he positioned himself above her; then she guided him into her and lifted her ass to thrust up onto him as he entered.

"Fuck," she sighed. "Fuck, hon, that feels good."

She was wet and slick and ready, her pussy holding his cock firm and resisting it just the right amount as he entered her all the way. Keith had been very, very close to climaxing when Shannon had been going to town on his cock. Now, though, he was past the point of sensitivity; utterly focused on fucking Shannon, he didn't think he could climax now if he tried. What felt good wasn't the physical sensation of his dick in her, but the experience of her naked body undulating against his as he drove into her. He liked it that way: he was going to hold back until the gorgeous little whore had as much as she could stand, and if he never came that was fine by him.

Keith began to fuck Shannon slowly, long slow thrusts deep

into her while she writhed and wriggled under him. He felt her surging with each thrust, felt the firmness of her pussy as she mounted quickly closer.

"Oh, god, hon," she moaned wildly. "Fuck, hon, I'm going to cum. You want to make your little whore cum? God, I'm going to cum so hard, your big cock is going to make me fucking cum, your big fucking cock is going to fucking make your little whore cum, hon, oh—ohhhhhhhh! OhHHhaahahHHHhhhhhh!!!" She screamed wildly as she fucked up against him, pounding herself against the bed violently. Keith had figured out by the second "big cock" that Shannon was faking, and faking inexpertly, because that was fucking hot—she was a whore working a trick, and strangely enough it made Keith hot that she was faking so loudly—especially because he could feel from the way her body reacted that she was not that far from actually coming.

He pulled out of her while she was still faking. She looked up at him and panted, "What's wrong, hon?"

"Roll over," he growled.

"Ooh," she said. "Are you coming in my back door already?" She wriggled her legs up in front of him and then flipped, spreading her legs around him and lifting her ass up high in the air, displaying her pussy and asshole.

"Not yet," he said, but got the lube just in case. He set it next to them on the bed and grabbed her hips firmly, lifting her ass up in the air to take her. He fitted his cockhead to her slit and worked it up and down; when she reached back to put it in, he gently pushed her hand away and then took firm hold of her hips as she tried to push onto him.

"Do you know what I do with whores who fake orgasms?" he growled.

Shannon looked back at him, her bright blue eyes rich with excitement. Her voice was like chocolate.

"What, hon? What do you do with whores who fake it?" She tried to ease herself onto his cock and he held her hips there firmly, not letting her mount him but keeping his cock right at her entrance. He began to enter her.

"Ohhhh—apparently you fuck the shit out of them, hon, oh, hon, you're making me cum again! Ohhhh ohhhhh—aaaaaha-HAAHAHAHHA!" She was really enjoying herself now, playing the part of the shameless whore, getting off on faking loudly as much as she would have gotten off on a real orgasm—almost. Keith raised his hand.

She didn't even see it coming. His hand came down so fast that the cracking sound of his open palm hitting her ass hit her before the sensation of being spanked. As the sharp sting flooded her body, Shannon looked shocked, then pleased, then overwhelmed.

"Ooh, hon," she laughed. "Hon likes to play!"

He cut off her moans with a much harder blow to her apple-cheeked ass; she regarded him over her shoulder with a look of surprise.

"Ow, hon," she said. "That hurts!"

He reached out and put his hand in her hair, pulling her head back firmly. The new cut offered less to hang on to, but was easier to get a hold on.

He pulled Shannon's hair. He spanked her hard. She yelped, then moaned. He spanked her again. She pouted over her shoulder at him, trying to turn her head, but he held her hair firmly and smacked her ass harder than ever. Her flirtatious pout went away in an instant and became a surprised O of sensation.

Holding her head so he could look in her blue eyes, he wedged his knee against her thigh and forced her legs open wider. Her lips went tight together and she made an *MMMMMmmm* sound as he did that, because it made her sink down onto the bed and onto his cock. But that's not why he did it. He wanted to get a better shot at that perfect curve right where her ass became the backs of her upper thighs. He put his fingertips there and caressed, then pressed. Shannon moaned softly as she realized what he was about to do. Her sweet spot was already hot from the spanks he'd delivered so far, but it was about to get a hell of a lot hotter. He held her hair tight so she could look at him as he raised his hand and got ready to deliver.

He thrust his cock deep inside her, so that her fake-blue eyes went wide and then her mouth popped open. He held her hair tight to keep eye contact as he worked on the sweet spot on one side of her ass.

He started spanking her rhythmically. She writhed against him, her nude body shuddering all over as she reacted to his thrusts and blows. He kept fucking her as he smacked the curve of her ass slowly at first, driving his cock into her with each stroke, making sure that the thrusts of his cock perfectly matched the blows to her sweet spot which, Keith knew from experience, sent hot vibrations right into Shannon's clit. She got an excited look on her face as she started to realize what her trick was up to. Keith had been planning to fuck her from behind and reach around to work her clit, but with Shannon's cheeky little act he'd decided there were better ways to make her stop faking. Shannon knew it, and the sight of that knowledge flaring in her eyes made Keith's cock harder and made him spank her harder as he fucked her, driving deep as he punished her perfect pale ass.

Shannon's lips trembled and she let out a soft groaning sound as she realized that it was really going to happen: Keith was going to spank and fuck her until she came.

She tried to play along with her previous game, wailing "Yeah, hon, you're going to make me cum, hon—" but couldn't keep it going because her eyes kept rolling back in her head and she kept losing control over her lips as they opened in wild uncontrolled sounds. The best she could do was to gasp things about his big cock as she mounted toward orgasm—then there wasn't anything she could do but fuck back onto him and moan.

He picked up the pace as Shannon's hips worked with greater urgency; he could tell that she was losing it, right on the verge of a huge climax. He had to let go of her hair so he could work on both sides. He hit her twin sweet spots, usually just one but now spread gorgeously around his cock, with decreasing sting and increasing thud. Shannon's head sank onto the starched white pillow and she turned just enough to keep eye contact with Keith as her eyes went wet and open with impending orgasm. Her lips trembled and she uttered a sudden uncontrolled cry as her sex began to spasm on his cock. Then her whole body went taut and she pushed herself up onto her hands and knees, fucking herself hungrily back onto him.

As her orgasm raged through her, he finished spanking her and grabbed her hair again, surging down onto her, pinning her to the bed. He bit the back of her neck and pounded into her, and Shannon uttered rapturous noises as he fucked her. Then, just as she was sinking into afterglow mode, he pulled out of her.

He got back up on his knees and leaned back, reaching for the lube. Her eyes went wide as she remembered what was coming next.

"Oh, god, hon, you're really going to take my ass, aren't you? Ohhhhh...god, be gentle, hon, it's my first time..." It wasn't, but that was hardly the point.

He slid off the bed and bent over the edge of it, parting Shannon's cheeks and planting his mouth hungrily between them. She let out a shocked noise and shivered all over; this seemed to be the last thing she expected. He'd never licked her ass; but then again, if she was going to dress up like a hooker then it seemed like a soft slow rim job was just sort of tit for tat.

His tongue found the tight pucker of her hole and began to swirl around; she clutched the bed as he worked her asshole and slid two fingers into her sex. She was still spasming from her orgasm; he could feel the muscle contractions growing stronger as he licked his way up and down her crack, focusing on the tight hole he was about to violate. As her pleasured sounds got louder, he used his thumb to tease her clit, and he felt her pussy tightening against his fingers as he got his tongue as deep as it would go into Shannon's back door. He went from lick to thrust, fingering her pussy as she got more excited, as the tightness of her hole began to relax. She started uttering whore pleas again, begging hon to fuck her ass. He lifted his face from her ass and got on his knees behind her. He broke open the lube packet and drizzled it over his cock, then into her crack. Shannon moaned as he worked one, then two fingers into her asshole. She felt tight but ready. He guided his slick cockhead up to her rear entrance and began to work it in.

"Oh, fuck," he gasped as the head popped in to Shannon's ass. "Oh, my god that's tight."

"First time, hon," she moaned breathlessly as he slid into her ass. Her words trembled with the saying and she wasn't faking the whore voice anymore: "I'm going to get off again."

"I can't fuck you very hard," he said, grinding his cock in and out of her in tiny little one-inch thrusts. "Or I'm finished." He'd been close already, but now he was right on the edge. A few long strokes into Shannon's asshole, and Keith really was going to climax.

"Then don't fuck me," she said quickly. Her hand went to her clit and she started rubbing rapidly in circles. "Just hold still. Hold still… Oh, god, oh, fucking god…"

Her ass was so tight, and his cock so deep inside it, that he could feel every stroke of her hand pulling against her flesh; he could also feel the spasms begin, seemingly even before Shannon knew they were coming. She certainly sounded shocked when the orgasm began to explode through her, making her asshole tighten rhythmically as she stopped rubbing her clit and clawed at the cheap bedspread.

The spasms of Shannon's ass were more than Keith could take. He uttered a groan and let himself go, thrusting deep into her. She moaned and reached back, holding her cheeks as he came inside her. The pleasure was intense; he'd been so hot for so long that it started deep in his body and pulsed outward deliciously. He gave a long, low sigh as he finished, and then slid on top of Shannon, his cock popping out as he relaxed.

He kissed the back of her neck. "So this was your meeting at South Station, eh?"

"Actually, it was more of a date," she sighed. "And I've got another one next Friday, too."

"Oh, you're going to make a habit of this?"

She wriggled out from under him, rolled onto her side, and put her arms around him.

"Not exactly," she said. "Next week's date's at the Plaza Hotel." She ran her hand down his chest, narrowing her eyes and sizing him up.

"How do you think you'd look in a tux?" she asked.

KNIT ONE, PURL TWO

Jacqueline Applebee

Cast On:

I am a man, and I'm not ashamed to say that I love to knit. I know it's strange, but believe me when I tell you that I am not secretly gay, I do not wish I were a woman, and I am not weirder than you. It's just that I like my needlecraft.

Sometimes people come over and talk to me about their grandmothers who used to make baby clothes, but mostly I just get stared at. I suppose that folks aren't used to seeing a man do this kind of thing. Myself, I'm never happier than when I'm surrounded by my wool. I love the feel, I love the look, and I love the sounds—the gentle *click-clack* of knitting needles that plays like music when I really get into it.

Now that's sorted, let me tell you about my first taste of bondage.

I met up with a few fellow knitters last Thursday at an anarchist bookshop-cum-café in South London. We were all supposed to be working on a joint project—a collage made of reclaimed materials that would eventually decorate the bare walls. I was distracted by a long blue scarf that I was finishing off, which in turn was taking my attention away from a sparkly purple hat that I was supposed to be knitting for my girlfriend, Eve.

That day I sat surrounded by weird and wonderful material, when I noticed that three people were seated opposite, all watching my small group with open wonder. Two women, one black, one white, and a thin young man sat huddled together. They pointed wordlessly, and tilted their heads to appreciate the view. I held up the unfinished blue scarf that I was working on, and three mouths smiled at me.

I got talking to Lindy about the new rabbit she'd taken in—she was knitting lengths of bright white plastic. I shared a sticky carrot cake with Brian, who was crocheting a circle made of black ribbons, and then I turned back to my ever-growing scarf. I entered that special place where it was just the yarn, the needles, and me.

The next time I looked up to the threesome, they were huddled close together. They shared a three-way kiss that left me wondering what it would feel like to be the man in the middle. I spied hands discreetly stroking his thighs and then move higher to his stomach. The thin man held up his hands, and it was then that I noticed that they were bound with shiny brown tape. The blonde woman in front inched away from the man as he tried to lean toward her. The black woman behind him captured his bound hands, holding them over his head so that he was somewhat immobilized.

Click-clack, click, click; my needles danced in my hands. Seeing these happy people made me feel so alone, even though I had two good friends next to me. I wished that my long scarf could reach across the country to where Eve was. Would my

dropped stitches let her slip away? I missed my girlfriend so
much right then.

I felt as if I were being taunted. The guy in the middle still had
his hands bound, and he still had a smile on his face as if this was
where he was supposed to be—trapped between two women. The
blonde grabbed his chin and drew him into a kiss, a messy and
brutal kiss. The black girl held him fast from behind, but I still
saw her hands sneak around to the man's crotch. I became aware
of my own groin, of the tightness I could feel, the wet spot that
suddenly appeared. My fingers could not stop moving; they kept
pace with the three cavorting lovers across the room from me.

The lucky sod was groaning, though I couldn't really hear
him; I could see his mouth open as the women took turns playfully pinching him. My yarn became tangled in my lap. I was
caught in a web of confusing thoughts. *How did they all get
together? Why don't I ever meet people like that? How does
it feel to be tied up?* The last thought made my needles slip,
and I almost stabbed my arm; I held it up to see an angry red
scratch over my pale pink skin. I'd never wanted to try anything
like that before. I looked up from my pile of knitting, and I
realized that things had progressed. The black girl kissed her
lover's neck, the blonde girl stroked his arm, and the man...the
man was looking directly at me. I dropped my knitting with the
shock of it. I glanced up once more, and he smiled at me in a
friendly way. There was no challenge, no anger, just a look of
bliss that he seemed to want to share. I felt myself blush, and my
cock twitched in my jeans. I clutched a ball of yellow wool to
reassure myself, wondering where all the oxygen had just gone.

"Mate, are you okay?" Brian's voice sounded far away,
although he was right next to me. I nodded and tried to uncross
my eyes.

"I'm great. I'm fine."

* * *

I spoke to no one about it. My hands were restless, still knit-ting furiously days later. I had finished my scarf, all eight feet of it, by the time Eve came down from Bristol at the weekend. I love Eve—she's a calming influence that makes me relaxed right down to my bones. Eve's coloring is dark strong chocolate, but she tastes twice as sweet.

I saw blurred movement from the corner of my eyes as she bustled around my room, opening windows, letting fresh air into the space that I had locked myself away in. Finally she settled between my sprawled legs.

"What's wrong, Danny?"

I couldn't speak for a moment; I just held out the long blue scarf to her, and when she took it from me, my arms remained outstretched.

"Please." I could barely get the words out. Eve looked up at me, and I bit my lip. "Please tie me up." I was aware of how squeaky my voice had become.

Eve looked down at the scarf as it lay in her arms, and then back up at me, eyes wide with shock.

"Excuse me?"

"Please, baby," I almost begged.

"Are you sure about this?" Eve tilted her head and assessed me for a moment. Then in a burst of energy, she leaned up and kissed me, a hot, hungry kiss. I knew I was a selfish, greedy bastard, but I still wanted to feel another pair of lips on me, wanted to feel two sets of hands holding me before I fell apart. Eve broke the kiss, and her dark brown lips were swollen and wet. Her nipples peeked through her thin top. She looked so beautiful.

I really should have knitted that hat for her.

I held out my arms once more, and thank god, she finally did something. The yarn was soft at first; I had felt it slip through my fingers as I was knitting the scarf, but as it swept over my forearms and wrists now, it was completely different. Eve was no expert, but she had me secure enough in a few quick minutes. It was exhilarating; my hands were now a separate part of me. I couldn't speak properly—I panicked for a moment, wondering what I had done. But all of my thoughts disappeared when Eve yanked opposite ends of the scarf, and it was suddenly pulled tight. My head fell back, and I groaned out loud. It felt so good, it was untrue. I flexed my wrists and felt the sting of every single loop. It was bliss. Eve reached into my bag, pulled out more and more wool. She slid down to my ankles and bound my bare feet together.

I loved this woman; I wanted her to cocoon me, to hold me in a web, and we'd see what kind of creature emerged later. Eve's eyes were wide, her face open, watching me as I writhed about like a bug caught in a spider's trap.

"I always knew," her voice was a whisper. "I knew you had this inside you." I looked away for a second, and then glanced back as Eve peeled off her sweaty top. She wasn't wearing a bra—her nipples were dark, stiff, and a sight to behold.

"Get on your knees," she ordered.

A split second later, I knelt on the sofa, my bound hands dangling over the back. If she knew I had this inside me, I wished she would have let me know. I had learnt a lot this week, another thing being just how sharp Eve's fingernails were. She reached beneath my jumper and raked her fingers over my back. I grunted and twitched like crazy. We weaved together, two bodies forming patterns of desire. Eve scratched me harder. I did not struggle—I was where I belonged. I almost sobbed as she kissed my bruised flesh. She snaked her hand to my front and jammed it inside my jeans, puffing out a breath as she fought her way into the restricted space between my legs.

"Do you want me to bind your cock?"

I didn't think I could respond to her offer with words alone, so I arched myself against her, rubbing my backside against her crotch. Eve did a sterling job of tugging my jeans down to my knees. My boxers came down with another yank. I felt like a single touch would make me explode. She ran a length of yarn under my balls—I looked down and recognized it as the sparkly material I was going to use to knit her hat with. I felt the ticklish pull of the fiber, the stinging tug of my pubic hairs that tangled in the threads. The purple glittery yarn stood out in contrast to my flushed skin, but against Eve's dark brown fingers, it looked wonderful. My body felt like one giant nerve ending, but my restrained balls held me back from coming. I never dreamed that I'd have this kind of reaction to being tied up.

The next thing that Eve did was to press a huge ball of emerald green wool against my dick. I surged into the plush softness. I didn't know what the hell I looked like, but I imagined it must be pretty strange—a grown man humping a ball of wool, and bound with lengths of yarn. It must be a bit mad.

"Up you get," Eve said, and then she helped me to hop in front of the full-length mirror by the door. I really did look like a freak, but I felt like a king.

Eve stood behind me, and she stroked my dick slow and steady as I rocked against her. Her fingers gripped tighter, a little at a time, and her hands moved faster, building up the intense pleasure I felt. I started to unravel as Eve held me up. She hooked two fingers into the wool that bound my balls, and she wrenched it off me in a single movement. I splattered the mirror—my come obscuring my own reflection as I jerked and cried out like a crazy person. I pictured the threesome from earlier in the week—they couldn't touch this, but I still had the image of more hands, more lips, and more sensation.

"Eve," I said breathlessly, "Eve I need to tell you something."

Eve murmured into my neck, and she started drawing swirls on my come-stained thighs with the tip of her finger. She lifted her hand to her mouth and sucked the fingertip inside, her eyes fixed on my mirror image the whole time.

"You are wonderful," I said, and I dropped the threesome fantasy like forgotten stitches.

After I cleaned myself up, I started working on Eve's hat. I chose a brand-new ball of wool to knit with, and soon the sound of *click-click, clacking* played like music in my mind.

Cast off.

MATINEE

Quinn Gabriel

Once upon a time, part of me would have been oddly thrilled by the blindfold. Once upon a time, I would have left work on the late shift and gone on a date without a second thought. But once upon a time, I was twenty and now I am not.

"We're almost there," Sam says in my ear. His lips are pressed to the fleshy curve and he nips me all of a sudden. It is unexpected and puzzling and a bright flash of white goes off behind the dark cloth covering my eyes. My eyes have given my pain color and light. I swallow a complaint because now I *am* oddly excited.

"Where are we?" I put my hands out and he immediately pushes them down. I'm blind and lost and completely at his mercy. I trust my boyfriend, but I don't like not knowing what he's up to. Or where I am. Or who might be watching. So now I'm exhausted and annoyed.

But my nipples are still hard and a pleasant sort of heat is between my legs. I stick my toe out and I feel his booted foot nudge it back into line. "Just walk, Cyn. Be a good girl. Don't make me spank you."

I freeze. My feet stall and my breath does, too. Where are we that he would say that out loud, and so confidently?

Sam and I have had our issues. We're rebuilding our relationship, our lives together. Mostly it's wonderful. Sometimes it's scary. Often it's dirty and the sex ranges from sweet to filthy. Sometimes I just want to punch him. Right now, I am thrashing in the wasteland of wanting to fuck him and wanting to punch him. Always a rule breaker, I can't choose just one.

Which is part of what led us here: to counseling, and reconnecting, and scheduled date nights. I had fucked around. Then so had he. A point for each side.

"Come on. Don't be such a brat." He pushes me, but I won't budge. I take a deep breath, shake my head, shut my eyes behind the blindfold.

Cool air kisses my face, very cool air blowing from overhead. Sam's fingers play lightly over my lower back. He rubs my waistband like a worry stone and I can hear the whisper of his fingertips over denim, but also something else—a hissing kind of feedback. I inhale again and breathe in the intense smell of popcorn: old stale popcorn, and fresh, hot and buttery popcorn.

I stick my leg out and he pushes it down again. "Brat."

"Be careful teasing me," I say softly. "I could start screaming *kidnapper* and you'll be eating dirt and getting cuffed before they figure out I actually belong to you."

What I mean is that we are married. But Sam laughs softly and leans into me. He presses his lips to my skin. My pulse beats heavily under his mouth. His voice is darker than I've ever heard it. "That's right. Don't forget it. You belong to me."

I open my mouth, trying to come up with some smartass remark to put him in his place, but I stop. I stop because his hand, hot and big, is cupping my pussy through my jeans. Nothing overt. He is resting his cupped hand over my mound, just touching me through my jeans.

"We're at the movies. But are we alone?" I breathe. I'm terrified that this man has me in front of a theater full of people and is touching me. Terrified and a bit hopeful. I shake my head and realize my knees are trembling. I feel like I might fall down if he doesn't hold me up.

His finger bends, strokes the split of my nether lips. He presses hard against my clit with the pad of his finger, driving the seam of my jeans against my flesh, rubbing me in front of what could be an empty theater or a jam-packed one. My breath stutters in my chest and I fear I might cry.

"That's for me to know and you to find out, Cyn. But only if you're a good girl."

The cruel part of him would put me on display. Cruel but proud. I think part of him would gladly show me off. The things he does to me. The things I let him do. The way we can be together, fast and nearly destructive like a flash fire. "I'll be good."

I have no choice. He leads me like his pet up a set of steps. It takes everything I have in me to follow. To behave. I have to go slow and hold on to him and trust him or I will fall. I don't want to fall. I like to be in control. Until the time when I don't, and then I want to hand myself over to Sam. Right now, I would give every dollar in my wallet to rip off the blindfold and see. But I won't. I'll be good. For his sake. For *our* sake.

"One more." He tugs my hand and I follow. My heel catches on the carpet and I stumble before he grabs me and keeps me from going down.

My heart hurts from beating so hard. "Thanks."

His lips are on me then, crushing against mine, nipping and licking, and his tongue fills my mouth. His hand is back over my pussy, and his finger is pressing, pressing, pressing until a soft pink sparkle blooms behind the blindfold. More color in my blind vision.

"Sit down," he says. I reach out to feel a seat but there is no seat. He is pushing me down on the step. "Right here is fine, Cyn. Be a good girl and give up control."

That was what our therapist had said. Sorry. Not therapist: "marriage coach." *You are still controlling, Cyn, when you are the one demanding that he take control. You are giving up your control, which forces Sam to be the one who takes it. Let Sam choose when he is in control.*

My thought at the time had been, *Over my dead body.* But I had smiled and said I understood.

Right now, I want to be in control. And he sees this. Because as I give in to my urge and reach for the blindfold, he gathers my hand in his. His touch is harsh and he pushes my hands together behind my back and binds me. I don't know with what, but the fabric is soft. I twist my wrists. The binding is soft but strong.

He pops my mouth open with his big fingers and I open for him like a rare flower. My lips pout out and without thinking I explore the air in front of me with my tongue like a snake. His zipper sounds and the warm head of his cock brushes my lips. He's making me do this. He is taking my control from me. He is in charge. I suck him into my mouth with a sigh.

He's velvety smooth and hot on my tongue. I can taste our shower gel on his skin and the salty tang of warm man. He laughs and pushes harder into me. He's not being gentle, and he's not being kind. I shift on the hard step. I'm wet and I'm ready, and I want so bad to beg but I can't seem to do it.

I hear someone coughing, and I freeze. But he fucks my mouth like I haven't stopped. I hear the projector jump to life and the booming soundtrack of coming attractions. Lights skitter over the darkness that cloaks my eyes and I wonder again. *Where are we? Who is here? Do I care now?* After all, I have his dick in my mouth in public. For all I know, I'm surrounded by a roomful of men. I shiver and shift again. God help me, I like the thought.

I would deserve that as penance. Wouldn't I?

"That's it, baby." This is all he says. I listen for more coughing. More sounds. More clues. I try to feel my surroundings. Beyond the music of a calliope and the bright lights painting streaks behind the blindfold I am lost.

He gives me a moment where he's not pushing my head, and I take a deep hiccupping breath. I manage to blurt, "Where are we? What is the movie?"

My brain ticks it off. The Beltway? The Senator? The generic big movie house that's in the city?

"Oh, I'm ashamed of you, Cynthia. Our first movie together. I thought you would get that if you listened. I'm afraid you'll need to pay for your lack of observation." He grips my skin with hard fingers, punishes me with his soft words, gentle tone.

My mouth opens again. Closes. I want to bitch and complain and say no. Instead I rise when he pulls me. He pushes me over like he's frisking me. His cop sensibilities take over. He pushes my legs apart, runs the blade of his hand up the inside of my thigh. He briefly cups my pussy in his big hand, and I have to bite my tongue to stifle my cries. He is so very in control in his world, but in mine, I am the one who cracks the whip. He may have a gun but I have control.

But not tonight.

He slides his fingers over the seam of my jeans, across my waist, up my torso. He pinches my nipples and briefly rings my throat with the huge circle of his hands. It is almost malicious, that gesture, but the touch is gentle. "Cyn, Cyn, Cyn. What do you hear?"

I hear the music of a carnival or boardwalk. Men's voices and a woman. No. Not men. Boys. Boys' voices and a woman. I know that voice. I do.

"I hear boys. And a woman. A mom it sounds like and I hear..." I can almost hear the click in my mind. I grin. I laugh. And then I sigh because he's reached around me, his big arms encompassing me, and he's dealing with my jeans.

"Good girl. You are a good student. You get a reward."

My reward is that my jeans are yanked down and so are my panties, canary yellow silk ones that I wore because they make me cheerful. My reward is his big fingers pushing into me and the feel of his hard-on pressed to the cleft of my ass. My reward also includes his teeth, white and sharp, pressing to the back of my neck until the muscles in my stomach flutter with excitement.

I blurt out the name of the movie like a prayer said aloud. I chant it, repeating the name over and over again as he thrusts against my ass, fucking me with his fingers.

"Good, girl. Good, Cyn. Are you ready? Because I'm going to fuck you. Right...here."

I'm still again, my breath harsh. That means what? Right here in front of everyone? Right here in the open? Right here in front of our movie? Right here...just us?

He parts me with his fingers, and I'm dripping wet at all the possibilities. Big men leering at us in the dark flickering light as he fucks me. A solitary watcher in the back, watching me be fucked, jerking his cock in time to our actions. Just us, tiny and silhouetted by the oversized, larger-than-life shadows of a film? All of it is good. Any of it is good. I spread my thighs and let him open me up, part me like a sea of flesh and blood. I am dripping.

My brain shoots me a memo. "Our movie. The movie. Was

only a matinee." I say it in little puffs because he is three fingers deep in me now.

"Tony runs the camera. He arranged a midnight matinee. I asked him nice." Sam pushes the bundle of nerves that are my G-spot, and I whimper like I'm dying.

Tony is his friend. Tony likes money. Sam is not afraid of paying for things.

"Our own matinee." I would be flattered, but he's moving me. Pushing and propelling me until I'm up against the wall. I know it's the wall because the carpet rubs my ass and my head bangs the thick padding—ping-ponging, ricocheting. Moving at his will. A scary and wonderful vertigo overtakes me and I am at his mercy. I let my thighs fall open and my husband, my Sam, puts my bound wrists over his head. Lets them fall around his neck. "Put your arms around me like you love me, Cyn. Like you need me." His cock slides between my thighs then.

He's in me and he's fucking me, with angry quick jerks that turn my blindness red and make me gasp with each forceful thrust. Of course I love him. Of course I need him. Doesn't he know that? And then I realize he doesn't. He does not know.

I push back against him. All of me softened. All of me sorry. All of me ready and wet and hot. I wrap my leg around his waist, draw him in. Find his mouth with mine and kiss him. I'm so sorry. I kiss my penance.

We grow still. The big voices and big lights fill the theater.

Then Sam moves in me. Harder. Faster. Nearly cruel with his motions but I take it all. Part for him. Open for him. Draw him close and take his punishment. His teeth at my neck. His words in my ear. *Cold, bitch, love, life, need, hate, keep, have...forever.* I take all the words and all the thrusts and nod. I smile behind my blindfold and I press back against him; my arms around his neck, my fingers playing in his dark hair. I drive my back into the cheap rough carpet and in my mind we are alone. We are surrounded. We are watched from above. We are secluded.

It shifts and changes, constantly rolling like a fog bank. He is cupping my breasts, pinching my nipples, stroking my flanks, and I am coming. In the painted black-and-white of the theater. With the checkered, torn, and quilted past we share.

I am coming and he is coming with me, his fingers in my long brown hair and then pinching my ass. Circling my waist, stroking my thigh.

"Touch me like you need me, Cyn. Make me believe it."

"I need you, Sam." I dig a fingernail into his skin. I push my body against his, taking his cock, thrusting my hips. "I need you. Believe it."

On the screen I hear, *I'm at the mercy of your sex glands, bud.*

And I'm coming again behind the blindfold. Maybe alone with him. Maybe on show. But safe. With the sparks of light and realization. My own personal dark. My midnight matinee.

BLACK LIGHT

N. T. Morley

Seeking refuge from the party, Jana had planted herself on the red velvet couch with a beer and was watching an abstract dance of glowing neon shapes on the forty-two-inch plasma with the White Stripes blaring on the stereo. Miles came up behind her.

He leaned over the back of the couch, bent down, and let his arms curve over her shoulders, hands resting on her breasts. He kissed her and she arched her back, then said, "Hey!" when he began to gently finger her nipples.

"Everyone else is getting comfortable."

"Yeah, I know," she said, relaxing into the couch and letting him kiss her again. His fingertips caressed her some more and she started to wish she'd worn a bra—kind of. Her nipples hardened at his touch and she sort of wanted more; glancing around, she saw people sprawled around making out, one chick with two guys, even. Terry and Tina's parties were always like this, and it never felt sleazy. She relaxed into it and as he kissed her she even let him slide his hands down her shirt. If he hadn't noticed before that she wasn't wearing a bra, he realized it now, and seemed to approve.

She drew the line when he slid his hand down to her thigh and started moving it up, though. She was not wearing anything down there, either, and in her current mood, she'd definitely end up begging Miles to fuck her from behind on the couch, in front of everyone. Jana gently closed her thighs, kissed Miles on the lips, and said softly, "Wouldn't you rather go somewhere more private?"

He disengaged from her, came around to the front of the couch, and eased himself down next to Jana, taking her in his arms.

"Yes, I think so," he said. "How about here?"

His lips on hers were just the right amount of firm and his tongue was just the right amount of soft; so right, in fact, that when his hand went up her skirt she spread her legs a little, and when he lifted her shirt to expose her teacup breasts, she let him. He bent low and began to suckle her hardening nipples; she felt a thrill as she wondered if he was going to go down on her right here, with everyone watching. She decided she was going to let him; in fact, if he wanted to fuck her, here, everyone would get to see it. They were definitely collecting some spectators, and some make-out sessions had stopped or slowed down to allow the participants to watch them. Jana felt scared but turned on; fuck it, she was going to beg him for it.

This time when he moved his hand under her short skirt she not only let him but whimpered a little, nipping at his tongue as he discovered that a bra wasn't the only thing she'd gone without.

"You little devil," he whispered as he caressed her smooth, bare pussy. He slid two fingers into her and discovered she was not only bare and shaved, but wet.

She let out a vixenish "Ah!" and snuggled her body more tightly against him, adjusting her hips to push herself onto his fingers. He thumbed her clit and she arched her back, whimpering; he pressed deeper into her and she looked up at him hungrily.

"I found a place," he said. "I think you'll like it."

"What's wrong with right here?"

"Too many spectators," he said; though plenty of people were sprawled around making out, several were eyeballing them with a mix of eagerness and distaste. "This one's more private."

He pushed his fingers more fully into her, and she gasped, whimpered, moaned softly, and said, "I'm game."

He slid his fingers out of her and brought them to her lips; she obediently licked them clean. She could never say no to Miles. He took her hand, guided her to her feet, and began to lead her out of the living room into a hallway. She was already in the hall when she realized her top was still pulled up; when she went to pull it down he put his big arm around her from behind and held it up, showing her off to everyone she passed. People paused while making out to look appreciatively at her breasts, especially as Miles fingered her hard nipples. She breathed harder with every step.

"It's official," she said. "You've made me the biggest slut at a Terry and Tina party."

He chuckled, his breath warm in her ear. "Not yet I haven't," he said, his voice like melted chocolate. "But I'm about to."

Miles led her into a back bedroom that looked totally dark from the hall. As he guided her into it, she saw that it wasn't totally dark; there was a faint blue-purple glow, and the walls were streaked with glowing shapes. A trio of partygoers—two girls and a guy, she thought—were parked on a big bunch of pillows, giggling and rubbing one another's bellies, arms and legs with phosphorescent paint, their fingertips leaving streaks as they played. The pillows, too, were smeared with glowing colors.

The trio looked up as Miles and Jana entered; their eyes lazed over Jana's now faintly glowing breasts and they smiled.

"You don't mind, do you?" asked Miles.

"Nah," said one of the chicks, standing. "We were just leaving." Miles pulled Jana close and kissed her as the three filed past them with knowing glances. Miles got a hold on Jana's top and pulled it up farther; she obediently lifted her arms and let him pull it over her head. A sudden attack of shyness made her cross her arms over her breasts as Miles tried to caress them.

"What's the deal?" she giggled.

Miles smiled, kissed her, and pushed her back. She went easily down onto the big pile of pillows, laughing a little as she did. She propped herself with her arms behind her and let Miles watch her for a moment, thrilling at his appreciative look. She kicked off her shoes and gave Miles a smile. Miles turned and closed the door, locking it. He took off his own shirt, grabbed a ketchup bottle from somewhere, and joined Jana on the pillows. She gasped and descended into hysterics as he upended the ketchup bottle and squirted a thick stream of glowing yellow liquid onto her breasts; it was cold.

"Black light," he said. "And neon paint. *Edible* neon paint," he said, and leaned down to lick it off of her.

"Huh?" Jana giggled. "No way. Edible? Nothing like a little radium in your diet...." Miles's lips closed over her hard yellow nipple, and she moaned as he suckled. She arched her back and reached down to slide her skirt off of her body; since she'd already kicked off her shoes, she was totally fucking stark naked, and she knew she was about to get fucked.

Hungrily, she reached out for Miles's belt buckle, but he guided her hand away and squirted more paint on her body. The cold made her gasp; she squirmed under his stroke as Miles smeared the thick glowing yellow paint over her breasts, illuminating them. He continued down her belly, coating her in neon, and when he tugged gently on her thighs she obediently opened them, exposing her sex.

He reached out and grabbed the pink paint—same kind of ketchup bottle. He kissed her deep and squirted cold liquid on her thighs, smearing and caressing it all over her pussy.

"You're sure it's edible?"

"And sugar free," he said. "No artificial sweeteners—that's why it tastes so good." He slid his glowing fingers into her mouth. The taste was kind of chalky and a little gross, except she could still taste her pussy, which made her go all wet inside. She opened her legs farther, and he drew his fingers from her mouth, taking them to her pussy, teasing it open. She moaned as his fingers slid into her; she clutched him close and wriggled against his stroke. The soft glow suffused the room, Jana's breasts phosphorescing as they surged with each little moan and twitch of her body.

"And everyone can see," Miles said into her ear, his thumb working her clit.

It took her a moment to realize what he'd said; by then, he had slid three fingers into her, out, in again, then out; she'd already undone his belt buckle and had his cock out and was about to bend forward to take it in her mouth. She was moments from his cock and both of them smeared with paint, when it dawned on her what he'd just said.

"What?"

He looked puzzled. "Everyone can see," he said. "You were watching."

With one orange-glowing hand, he gestured over to the webcam propped on a tripod, pointing right at them.

Jana panicked and stood. "The television?" she said. "Oh, fuck, you are fucking kidding me."

Miles took her wrist and tugged her back toward the pillows. "I thought you knew," he said. Jana turned toward the camera and looked down at her naked body, breasts smeared with glowing yellow paint, thighs and pussy smeared with pink.

"Sorry, I thought you knew," he said. "You were watching it."

"I couldn't fucking tell what it was," she said. "Or who it was."

Miles pulled her back onto him, and the fight went out of her as he said, "Neither can they."

She didn't have time to think about it—didn't *want* to think about it. She let him pull her into his lap and bend her over it, reaching down to finger her until she melted into his stroke. She lifted her ass high in the air and he teased her open and worked her clit; god, she wanted to fuck, and a few minutes ago she'd been about to give it up on the couch. He was hard against her, his cock hanging out and the tip as wet with precum as with glowing paint. "Fuck it," she said, and slid his pants off of him, leaving glowing streaks of light down his legs as she took his cock in her mouth and started sucking him.

His hands left streamers through her hair as he caressed her head gently; each time she looked up he was staring at the webcam, moaning with pleasure. That gave her a thrill, and when his breathing changed and she realized he would come if she didn't stop, she came off his cock, gasping and panting, and said, "Fuck it," again, then, "Fuck me." She left a pink hand-print in the center of his chest as she pushed him back onto the pillows, then turned around, climbed over him, and spread her legs very wide. She could feel his cock against her ass, and as she lifted herself slightly and guided it up against her pussy, she saw the wetness of her cunt making the paint run all over it. Soon Miles's cock was glowing, and as she teased herself open for him she got a visceral thrill wondering what the people in the living room were seeing. She stroked his cockhead against her opening and wriggled herself onto it; just like always, it made her gasp a little as it popped into her, then continued easily in as she settled down to take him all the way.

She felt the strain on her thighs as she began to fuck herself on Miles's cock. "Fuck," she heard herself saying. "Do people really fuck in this position?" Miles was too busy moaning in pleasure to answer, but as she looked down at her own naked body, glowing breasts, thighs, and pussy illuminated with Miles's big cock going into the latter, she thought, *Yeah, they do, when they're getting off on being watched.* She couldn't come like this; the curve of Miles's cock deep inside her just didn't hit the right spots, but god, how it fucking turned her on to see herself all aglow and exposed, naked as she fucked herself onto him with everyone in the living room watching. She could never come in public anyway, not when he'd fingered her at the movies or fucked her over the railing at the beach that one time, or when he'd gone down on her twice in that secluded corner in the back-yard at the Terry and Tina party last month. That didn't make her like it any less; in fact, she liked it more, because the plea-sure was purely exhibitionistic, and the physical part was just a fucking turn-on.

So she thought, as she fucked herself on Miles's cock—until she felt him lifting her off of him, turning her naked body over in his big arms, and flipping her onto her belly on the big pile of pillows. She stared into old fabric neon-streaked with a half-dozen colors as she obediently spread her legs and put her ass in the air, knowing she was about to get fucked. And with a mixture of panic and excitement, she understood that this was the position in which he always made her come.

She wasn't sure why—it was something about the angle, the way his cock went into her when she was opened wide and on her knees with her ass in the air, versus spread wide on her back, or riding him with her legs open facing in or facing out. All of those felt incredible, but it was this position, fucked from behind doggy-style, that always finished her off, even if she was trying to wait.

He got behind her, fitted his glowing cockhead to her pussy, and entered her with a sigh. She let out a sigh herself, taking him to the hilt, and she wriggled against him as he began to fuck her. She could feel the tension, the pressure of his cock hitting just the place it took to make her come; then he went up on one foot and tipped his body to the side, changing the angle. She puzzled over that for an instant, until she looked back and realized he was fucking her so the camera could see.

The smooth, easy pressure of cock to pussy was replaced by a shameless exhibitionistic thrill that made her understand that she was going to come anyway. Just in case, he reached down and began to stroke her clit, propelling her closer as she stared at the camera and thought of all those people watching, staring at her tits, her body, her spread thighs, her opened cunt.

That pushed her over the edge; her eyes rolled back and she came, moaning crazily, her lips forming a glowing O with the taste of the paint from his cock. She shuddered all over as he fucked her and rubbed her clit; her sex clenched tight around his cock and she sprawled helpless under him, her whole body suffused with light and pleasure.

He pulled out of her, rolled her over, and straddled her belly. She wrapped both her hands around his cock, eagerly prepared to jerk him off, but he wanted to do it, so he wrapped his hand over hers and stroked himself until with a cry of pleasure he shot warm cum all over her breasts, the spurts glowing, more faintly than the paint. She smeared it over her breasts, watching his cum mingle with pure light. Miles relaxed into the pillows next to Jana, kissing her, their naked bodies pressed together. Jana looked up and saw Miles's face, glowing with neon paint. Her own felt sticky.

She looked into the camera, picturing her own face, illuminated like Miles's—eminently recognizable, and brightly colored to boot.

So much for anonymity.

Jana kissed Miles deeply and spread her legs, sighing softly.

NIGHT SHIFT

Rita Winchester

I turned over and stared at the clock, beat my pillow, memorized the red numbers that glowed like fire: *3:11.*

Sleep was not coming. I knew that. It burned just under my skin. Restlessness. Worry. Anxiety. All mixed together, a toxic cocktail. Sleep was lost to me, and my heart beat with an unnamed fear. Too much in my head. I had two choices. I could make a cup of tea and wander the house alone, or I could distract myself.

I groped in the dark and found my cell phone. I flipped it open, started texting.

CAN'T SLEEP. YOU THERE?

It didn't take long. A minute or two and my phone belched out a little jingle that told me I had a text message.

RIGHT HERE. ALL ALONE. NEED SOME HELP?

I smiled. The smile held the fear and worry at bay just a little, enough that I felt some of the tension uncoil, felt a fluttering in my belly at nothing more than little blue words on a white screen.

ALWAYS. CAN I COME?

I hit SEND and closed my eyes. I let the anxiety sweep over me and then recede on its own. Like a tide, it moved over me, crushing me, receding, releasing me. It was awful but fixable.

The lilting jingle told me to check my phone.

I KNOW YOU CAN COME. YOU'VE PROVEN IT. GET UP HERE. I'M LONELY.

This time I laughed. I had proven my ability to come. Time and time again. I wanted to add one more instance of proof to the data.

BE RIGHT THERE.

I hit SEND and got dressed. It was cold out. I could hear the wind licking at the eaves of the roof, banging the metal awning outside my window restlessly like a war drum.

I headed out, dressed for cold but warm inside. The two-minute drive to the jewelry store was surreal: dark, deserted streets; the stoplights blinking their amber warning my only company. I knocked on the door and pressed my face to the frigid glass like a child. I felt like a child, a greedy little girl who wanted a treat and wanted it now.

Charlie opened the door without a word and pulled me to him, kissed me hard. I purred into his mouth and felt the tide of fear sweep a little farther out. Back out to the ocean of worry it had come from. His big hands dipped down the front of my jeans. Finding me absent of panties, he tickled my clit with the pad of his warm fingers. I squirmed against him, instantly going from damp to soaked, my pussy demanding more than a flick of his digits.

"I'm glad you came. I was very lonely. Not much to protect against at three a.m." His voice, rich and warm, licked at my ear and settled my nerves.

As always, the sight of him in his dark blue uniform did funny things to me; made me antsy and horny and hot for him. Not that I wasn't always that way, but the spiffy blue getup he was required to wear made everything more intense, like throwing kindling onto a burgeoning fire.

His fingers squirmed deeper, pushing into me, coaxing my cunt to grip around their strong warmth. "Wanna tell me what's wrong, Amy?"

I shook my head. No. I did not. Now was not the time for insecurities and money worries and crises of the soul. Now was the time for relief.

I took his free hand and pulled him back behind the glass counter. The diamonds and gold and silver he watched over until morning winked at me like co-conspirators. I glanced at the security camera and then at his smiling face.

"They still haven't gotten it fixed."

I pushed him to his knees and unbuttoned my jeans, sliding them down in one swift motion. Without a word, he buried his face at the V formed by my thighs, his tongue seeking and finding my swollen clit. He licked and sucked and swirled until my knees went weak. Then he lowered me, laid my thighs wide, and finished me off. He coaxed his rigid tongue into my cunt, reveled in the creamy prize that awaited him. He licked me clean until I was a writhing mass of pleasure who had forgotten the meaning of fear.

His zipper ripped the silence and I felt his swollen cock bump at me, nudge me, and then push me open. It demanded entrance that my body gladly gave. I opened around him then clamped on eagerly—not only my cunt but my entire being. I wrapped my legs around his sturdy hips and pulled him deeper, arched up to meet him, did my best to meld with him and become one. It wasn't possible but I gave it my all.

Charlie moved faster and buried his face in my neck. My

body pulsed and slammed against his, my cunt working at him in a frenzy. I was getting so tight, right there. He had me right there once again as if by magic. His cock jerked in me, grew a little longer, a little thicker. I was aware of every nuance and point of contact. He was going to come.

"Amy," he whispered, just my name, and then he bit me; the sweet, tender spot where my throat meets my shoulder.

My cunt spasmed around him. Long lovely spirals of pleasure coursed through me as I came around him and he came in me. "Sweet, sweet Amy. I love when you visit me."

I left him with a kiss, a promise to see him again soon. I went home and crawled into bed. The smell of him was still on my skin, his come sticky on my thighs. I slept.

SQUARE
LOOPHOLE

Craig J. Sorensen

Emily would be five feet tall in heels if she wore them. I'm six foot seven. She's pale as a full moon rimmed by silver clouds on a dark night. I'm dark as a dense tree's summer shadow in a blazing sunrise. Her corneas are so fair they are nearly seamless. Mine are black as onyx. Her body is full of round, soft, luxurious curves. Mine is stark and hard, appointed with sinewy muscles on a long, lean frame.

Of all our contrasts, these are not the most compelling.

Emily is modest. She wears her wavy, long blonde hair like a nun's habit. Her dresses and skirts are long and flowing, in muted dark tones. She never wears pants. She'd look right at home in a Victorian parlor, sipping Earl Grey.

From the first time I set foot on Black's Beach near San Diego, I knew there was no turning back. I love the sensation of the sun pouring down the length of my nude body. When I'm stuck in clothes, I like them tight and bright.

How could it be that two people so different both outwardly

and inwardly, could be drawn together? I speculate that we are yin and yang: perfected balance of light and dark.

It is customary that in the dark of night, beneath our covers, Emily peels away her nightgown and sensible panties to make love. Curtains and shades tightly sealed render barely enough light to illuminate the room. I rise up on my arms, and the outline of her body is tinted with the sparsest light. She combs her fingers into her long hair and pulls it over her head. She moans ever so softly as my tip finds her moist entrance.

It is a paint-by-number scene. Amidst consuming charcoal on black, my imagination fills the brush with the color of her skin recorded from her warmly freckled face when I playfully ease her hair back for a soft kiss on the back porch.

She pulls me tight. I study the lines of her face gently lit in the glowing blue of a small digital clock. "You're so beautiful, Emily."

Her urgent breaths cascade around my face, her fingers splay around my freshly shaved scalp and push our lips tighter, force me down from my midnight vista. My fingers become my eyes as usual while I recall her hidden terrain.

Sometimes I pull the covers back, one at a time. Comforter, blanket. I press my fingers to her hard clit to distract her and ease the sheet away. The reveal is like watching the moon rise on an obsidian night on the east coast of Baja; it would not be so dramatic with the sun in the sky. She bites her lip then grips the sheet with her toes and pulls it over my back.

A shiny fish disappears to the depths while I'm still trying to tie the lure on the line.

Her deep kiss and gripping fingers ambush me and she retrieves the blanket and the comforter and pulls them back up over us.

She feels so good.

* * *

I pad into the dining room to check the email, the shades still sealed against the burgeoning late spring dawn while Emily sleeps in. I start the computer then go to the dark kitchen to get a cup of coffee.

We've lived in this 1930s bungalow since we married last year, but just like Emily, it is still revealing new mysteries. As I fill my cup, I become aware of a sliver of bright sunlight behind me. I turn around slowly to see a vibrant mustard strip against the far wall.

The way the transom lies above the back door, pinched between a wall on one side and the dark walnut cupboards on the other, then capped by the ceiling of the porch on the outside, camouflages it. I look closely and am surprised at just how dingy it is.

Somehow Emily and I had missed it when washing the windows every time since we'd moved in. Judging from its current state, the last owners missed it too.

I study the light's brief path, a swatch of geometric yang in early morning yin. It blazes on the back wall cutting a path through the kitchen over the top of the pass-through bar into the dining room. A sliver of arrogant light, it defies the dense shades in every other window.

I never lie to Emily. She treasures truth more than her modesty. It takes all my will to appear sincere while I tell her I'm not feeling well, and that's why I'm not up for making love. I have to sleep on my stomach to keep my perpetually hard cock hidden. She's becoming suspicious by the third day.

Each morning, I rise early and measure the course of the sun through the dingy transom, which I dare not clean right now;

I have only one shot at this. I can hear it in her voice, feel it in the way she grabs my arm and tips her forehead against my shoulder. She needs to make love bad.

She tries to seduce me with her amazing, deep kisses in bed. She strokes my body and my cock stretches toward her. Her fingers collapse to it like a bear trap. "Feeling better, honey?"

"Not really."

The depth and quiver of her breath tell me more than words could. I can taste her frustration. "You sure? I could do all the— all the work." Her voice is a whisper.

Emily on top, I would be able to study her body down the dimly lit cave of our bed. No, do not be distracted! "Please, Em, I just need to rest."

"Fine." She rolls over and presents her back. She shows as much anger as I've ever seen from her. Mercifully, tomorrow the course of the sun will be perfect.

"What?" Emily's eyes open and fix. I lean against the bedroom doorway.

My cock is heavy, but I somehow contain its will to harden. "Come downstairs."

She leans on her elbow and sweeps her hand over her hair. The warm light of impending dawn makes tiny lines at the edges of the bedroom shades.

"Give me a minute, honey."

I've built it into my timeline. Emily will modestly put on a bra under her nightgown, relieve herself, brush her teeth and hair, cover with a long robe, and come downstairs, probably expecting I've prepared a special breakfast.

I have. I hope she will like it.

The transom is still dim when she arrives and looks around the dark, still kitchen. I don't dare look at it, as I hand her a cup of coffee. She sips then tilts her head. "What's going on?"

"I have a surprise."

When she focuses on her cup for a second sip, just the slightest edges of sun illuminate the diffused field of dinge on the transom. I place her coffee cup on the counter and gently kiss her.

She pulls back a bit when my cock presses her thigh. She looks around the room. Her pupils are so wide I could swim in them. Confusion grows on her face as I fold her hair behind her ears. The warm light grows, and I turn her around to show her the light through the transom.

Her breathing becomes short, her eyes turn my way but her face remains fixed forward. "What—do you—have in mind?" I turn her face to mine and I kiss her. I strip away my sweatpants and T-shirt. Her eyes widen as my hand traces between her breasts. I feel her pulse race as I begin to open her robe. Her arms fold briefly across her ribs, then drain away and she reluctantly lets me push the robe from her back. She stares at the transom.

"All the shades are drawn, Emily."

"But—"

I tractor the hem of her flannel nightgown up her legs bit by bit until it is gathered at her waist and her white panties glow in the ration from the reverse eclipse that burns startlingly bright.

She hesitates, shakes her head softly. I pull her two steps toward the stool. Her arms slowly rise over her head. I peel her nightgown. Her arms snap like springs over her bra and panties. She takes a deep breath through clenched teeth. A smile like I've never seen opens on her face. She looks at my cock, curling toward the ceiling. Her hoarse whisper is barely audible. "Oh, lord."

I unhook her bra, and again she hesitates. The light glows just above the level of her head on the back wall above and to the right of the stool, which I placed in the path. She relaxes and lets the bra fall away. I trace my fingers along the elastic at the top of her panties and playfully pull them. She follows another step. We push the panties down together.

Her pubic hair is as bright a gold as the shroud around her head. It's the first time I've seen it in the light. Her steps cross over each other modestly, then she mounts the stool. Her arctic white flesh glows warm in the fleeting light of the transom.

She crosses her legs. My lips graze hers and I trace my fingertips between her vise-grip thighs. Her legs and mouth open slowly like morning roses.

The golden light on her head lowers gently in coronation. I bow before her and remain between her legs. My eyes fix on the glow that slowly casts down her face. My tongue takes her hard wet clit into the front of my mouth.

There are twitches in her legs that imply she might want to run back upstairs and disappear into the modesty of dimly lit quilt and two blankets. But her moan is that deep, resonant sound she gets only when she must, must, must have sex. I reach my finger inside her and press at the front of her vagina. Her teeth glisten atop an immodest gaping jaw, her plump lips glow bright red to create a triangle with her blossoming cheeks.

I linger, tasting until sun's glow bathes her entire face. I feel the twitch of her legs, the sudden compression of her stomach that makes convulsive six-packs of her supple waist. "Oh, please make love to me."

"In time." My mouth returns to her vagina while my hands roam up her open thighs, fingers insert into her then trace her dew down to her knees. I continue to drink her, to watch the light of the transom cross over and light one breast. She surprises me by leaning to the side so both breasts are bathed in the glow that now has transformed to a bright gold, forming perfect crescent shadows on their sides. Her nipples are a bright pink, stiff and long with large budded rims. I've felt these details, seen their spectral monochrome images in the dim of the night. I resist the urge to touch. Only my eyes may devour this rare feast.

There is always time for touch later.

Emily writhes on the stool so hard the four legs clack like wooden wind chimes in a steady wind as my tongue enters her, then traces her slit. Her eyes connect with mine.

The light of the transom thins as the roofline deprives.

But the remaining light it rations into the kitchen lingers while I slowly, steadily drink Emily. Her legs spread so wide she is off balance. Her fingers coil to my shoulders to brace as she orgasms into my mouth.

"I need you inside me."

I stand and face her, she guides my cock inside her, and we make love, bodies crushed tight. I fight for every ounce of restraint to savor this moment. I come to the edge six times, but resist my need. Finally, lucky seven, I can resist no more. I explode so deep in Emily that her percussive breath compresses from her chest.

Face-to-face in the soft, fading gold light of the kitchen, we shudder.

The next time we clean the kitchen, Emily puts the stepladder by the back door, and she scrubs the transom. She looks back, pulls her locks from her face to expose her blush, and waits for me to confirm that it is clean.

In early summer, the sun will penetrate the transom at the perfect angle for just a few magic days.

The moon that is her modesty will defy its usual phases. Rationed sun will rise in all its glory when Emily and I meet in the kitchen for a rare breakfast feast. I know Emily and I will

never walk arm in arm nude down Black's Beach and that's fine
by me.

We know a light mighty as the sun.

THE AWAKENING

Jayne Pupek

Warm water rose around our hips and thighs. So soon the loofah and soap were abandoned, replaced by the easy movement of our bodies pouring into each other. All the splendid curves and angles found their perfect others. Against the white porcelain tub, we leaned and turned, our breasts floating, sinking, rising again, glazed with rain, with the sea, with the wetness of kisses.

Around us, blue walls receded, and everything beyond them vanished like long-ago dreams. Yesterday did not matter. Thoughts of tomorrow evaporated. There were only these moments and the urgency of discovery. Skin pressed against skin, and I thought: This is the moment of my awakening. I will never be the same woman, will never experience any subsequent moment without returning in some way to this one, singular and divine.

Limbs surrendered to the nothingness of bubbles, the rising of steam, the swirling hunger of tongues probing soft places. Who knew rapture existed in air tinged with lavender, in the necessary pull of hands, the eager opening of legs, in the reverberations of a voice chanting my name? Bliss, passion, Eros—these were words I'd seen on pages and heard tossed about like stones, but now they inhabited my cells and coursed through my blood. Even so, I knew no words could mirror what this woman ignited beneath my skin. A fierceness took hold inside the marrow of my bones. Longing burned inexplicably, even submerged in water, even as I held my breath and shook with ecstasy as radiant as light. Sighs fell like petals from Claire's soft mouth, and I succumbed to each one. Here I am, yes, always. Right here.

The night moved from the bath to the bed, and we moved with it, carried on waves like two ecstatic mermaids released into blue-green seas. We slept on foamy crests and swam in and out of each other's dreams. One moment we were slick-backed iguanas basking in the sun, nibbling on hibiscus leaves. Another, we were snails trailing each other's soft bellies. I kissed the pink shell of her ear, and thought how every conch keeps the sound of the sea inside, no matter how many miles inland the shell is moved.

The room came in and out of focus, swelling and receding like the sea itself. There were more droppers of warm milk and calamine dabbed on bites. More wine was opened and sipped first from glasses, then the bottle. Lights seeped through cracked blinds. Voices and car doors carried from the parking lot. We tossed and perspired and lost ourselves in sheets wet as new leaves. We wrestled like angels, and fell apart, exhausted, only to rise again, hands stroking awake the sleeper's tender thighs.

In drowsy moments, Claire traced my body with her fingers. Slow circles. Long lines. Her fingers claimed every crevice and plain, every blemish and scar. "Your flesh is the Braille I read," she whispered.

Yes, I thought. Read every story written on my body, every single word that came before this one, and the ones before that. Go back to the beginning with me, and know me as no one else has known me. Read every word you find in the days to come. And all the days beyond, until the words and days are all gone, and we expire like breath itself. Nothing left of us but the sound of each other lost in distant shells.

I looked up at the ceiling, at the cracks spreading like lines on a map to another world. If the roof opened, I knew the perfect sky would be littered with stars.

ABOUT THE AUTHORS

XAVIER ACTON is a geeky San Franciscan who strongly approves of short skirts and tube tops. His short stories have appeared in the *Sweet Life* series, *Slave to Love*, GoodVibes. com, TinyNibbles.com, GettingIt.com, *Luscious: Stories of Anal Eroticism*, and *Open for Business: Tales of Office Sex*, among others. Visit him at XavierActon.com.

RIC AMADEUS is the pseudonym of a veteran prankster who was deeply influenced by Falco as a child. Ric's work has appeared in *Juicy Erotica* and in the online zines Pump, Ugly Brigade, the Donner Party Newsletter, and underRATed.

JACQUELINE APPLEBEE is a black British bisexual writer who breaks down barriers with smut. She has had erotic stories included in several anthologies, including *Iridescence: Sensuous Shades of Lesbian Erotica*, *Best Women's Erotica 2008*, *Ultimate Lesbian Erotica 2008*, and *Best Lesbian Erotica 2008*.

Jacqueline also has a paranormal novella that includes sex with ghosts. Her website is at www.writing-in-shadows.co.uk.

RACHEL KRAMER BUSSEL (www.rachelkramerbussel.com) is an author, editor, blogger, and reading series host. She has edited or coedited over twenty books of erotica, including the companion volumes *Tasting Him* and *Tasting Her, Yes, Sir* and *Yes, Ma'am,* and *He's on Top* and *She's on Top,* as well as *Do Not Disturb: Hotel Sex Stories, Spanked, Naughty Spanking Stories from A to Z 1* and *2, Sex and Candy, Crossdressing, Dirty Girls, Rubber Sex,* and, with Alison Tyler, *Caught Looking* and *Hide and Seek.* Her nonfiction anthologies include *Best Sex Writing 2008* and *2009.* Her work has been published in more than one hundred anthologies, including *Best American Erotica 2004* and *2006,* Zane's *Chocolate Flava 2* and *Purple Panties, Everything You Know About Sex Is Wrong, Single State of the Union,* and *Desire: Women Write About Wanting.* She serves as senior editor at *Penthouse Variations* and wrote the popular "Lusty Lady" column for the *Village Voice.* Rachel has written for *AVN, Bust, Cosmopolitan, Curve,* Fresh Yarn, Gothamist, Huffington Post, Mediabistro, *Newsday, New York Post, Penthouse, Playgirl, San Francisco Chronicle, Tango,* TheFrisky.com, *Time Out New York,* and *Zink,* among others, and has appeared on "The Martha Stewart Show," "The Berman and Berman Show," and NY1. She has hosted In the Flesh Erotic Reading Series since October 2005, featuring writers such as Gael Greene, Maxim Jakubowski, M. J. Rose, and Zane. Rachel blogs at lustylady. blogspot.com and cupcakestakethecake.blogspot.com.

ANDREA DALE's stories have appeared in *Dirty Girls, The Mammoth Book of the Kama Sutra,* and *Naughty or Nice,* among others. With coauthors, she has sold novels to Cheek

Books (*A Little Night Music*, Sarah Dale) and Black Lace Books (*Cat Scratch Fever*, Sophie Mouette) and even more short stories. She still finds time to lounge in bed in the hopes that someone will bring her food. Her website is at www.cyvarwydd.com.

BELLA DEAN is new to the business of dirty stories. She still blushes when she types but has no plans to give up the job. She lives with her small family in her small house in her small town.

JEREMY EDWARDS has been frequently published online (at Clean Sheets and many other sites), and his work has appeared in more than twenty-five anthologies offered by Cleis Press, Xcite Books, and other print publishers. Drop in on him unannounced (and thereby catch him in his underwear) at http://jerotic.blogspot.com.

A. D. R. FORTE's erotic short fiction appears in various anthologies including *Best Women's Erotica 2008*, *Yes, Ma'am,* and *Hurts so Good*, all from Cleis Press. Her stories have also been featured in several Black Lace *Wicked Words* collections.

QUINN GABRIEL is a part-time writer and a full-time bad girl. She likes black boots, silver jewelry, old cars, and hot guys. When she's not pushing her porn, she works in a conservative office with uptight people. But she's not bitter.

ARIEL GRAHAM writes erotic fiction, science fiction, and nonfiction and spends the rest of her time reading and running. Her work can be found in the Cleis Press anthology *Frenzy*, on Ruthie's Club and Pink Flamingo websites, and in the anthologies *Call of the Dark*, *Bound to Love,* and *Witches' Night*. Ariel lives in Reno with her husband and multiple cats.

NIKKI MAGENNIS lives in Glasgow, Scotland, and is not very Zen. You can find her work in various anthologies from Cleis Press, including *Yes, Sir; Love at First Sting; E Is for Exotic;* and *J Is for Jealousy*, and in several of the Black Lace *Wicked Words* anthologies, including *Sex in Public* and *Sex with Strangers*, as well as in magazines and online. Her second erotic novel *The New Rakes* was published by Black Lace in November 2008. Visit her blog for haphazard updates: http://nikkimagennis.blogspot.com.

SOMMER MARSDEN's work has appeared in numerous anthologies. Some of her favorites include *I Is for Indecent, J Is for Jealousy, L Is for Leather, Spank Me, Tie Me Up, Whip Me, Ultimate Lesbian Erotica 08, Love at First Sting, Open for Business, Tasting Her,* and *Yes, Sir*. She lives in Maryland and keeps her alter ego to herself. Not really. She has a big mouth and knows how to use it. She has many addictions and has no intentions of getting help for any of them. They currently include red wine, writing smut, long walks, the downward dog position, emails, blog hopping, and biscotti. You can reach her at hot4sommer@yahoo.com or visit her at SmutGirl.blogspot.com to keep up with her dirty ramblings.

JASON MCFADDEN is the pen name of a San Francisco businessman who still gets a little thrill each time one of his stories makes it to print.

ZAEDRYN MEADE (www.zaedryn.com) is a queer butch activist, classically trained poet, spoken word performer, and smut writer. Her poetry and short stories can be found in various collections including NPR's "This I Believe" project and three *Best Lesbian Erotica* anthologies. Born and raised in the rainforest of Southeast Alaska, she now lives in New York City.

N. T. MORLEY is responsible for sixteen published novels of erotic dominance and submission, as well as several dozen published short stories and a double-anthology editing project, *MASTER/slave*. Morley's books include *The Parlor, The Limousine, The Circle, The Appointment, The Nightclub, The Visitor,* and the trilogies *The Castle, The Library,* and *The Office.* Find out more at www.ntmorley.com or email ntmorley@gmail.com.

JAYNE PUPEK is the author of the recently released novel, *Tomato Girl* (Algonquin Books) and a book of poems titled *Forms of Intercession* (Mayapple Press). She resides near Richmond, Virginia.

TERESA NOELLE ROBERTS gets paid to daydream about sex and romance. (She considers herself a very lucky woman.) Her erotic fiction has appeared or is forthcoming in *Caught Looking: Erotic Tales of Voyeurs and Exhibitionists, Hurts So Good, Spanked: Red-Cheeked Erotica, Dirty Girls, Succulent: Chocolate Flava 2, Yes, Sir* and *Yes, Ma'am, Rubber Sex,* and many other collections with titles that make her mother blush. She has published several novellas of erotic romance with Phaze Books and has also published in speculative fiction and several other genres.

Originally from England, **A. SILENUS** lives in Arizona where he writes nonfiction (mainly) for newspapers, magazines, websites, and occasionally books. His erotic short stories have appeared in *Forum* magazine in the United Kingdom, in the online Ruthie's Club, and in *The MILF Anthology,* published by Blue Moon Books. He recently completed an erotic novella set in southern England.

CRAIG J. SORENSEN's stories and poetry appear online at Clean Sheets and have been included in anthologies by Alison Tyler, Maxim Jakubowski, and Rachel Kramer Bussel. By day he busies himself in the information technology field. Visit him online at just-craig.blogspot.com.

SOPHIA VALENTI is an editor, writer, and lifelong New Yorker. She enjoys uncovering sexy secrets, attending sordid soirees, and writing all about them. If she's not reading or writing, she's probably drinking coffee. She hates spring cleaning but must confess that she most definitely has a passion for panties.

RITA WINCHESTER is a domestic goddess who likes to be tied up in her kitchen (or anywhere else). She is happily committed to one very sexy partner. Her work has cropped up in places like Ruthie's Club, The Erotic Woman, For the Girls, *I Is for Indecent*, and *Mammoth Lesbian Erotica*. You can drop her a line (or a rope) at Rita_Winchester@yahoo.com.

JORDANA WINTERS is a thirtysomething Canadian writer of women's erotica whose print credits include *Ultimate Sex*, *Best Women's Erotica 2008, 2007*, and *2006, Sex & Seduction*, *Uniform Sex*, and *Erotic Tales*. Her online credits include Tassels & Tales, A Woman's Goodnight, Lucrezia Magazine, Forbidden Publications, The Erotic Woman, Ruthie's Club, Oysters & Chocolate, Extasybooks, and Thermoerotic. When not hiding behind her computer telling filthy tales, Jordana is an often-disenchanted administrative whore. Email her at jordanawinters@yahoo.com or visit her: http://jordanawinters.tripod.com/.

KRISTINA WRIGHT's erotic fiction has appeared in more than fifty anthologies, including *Dirty Girls: Erotica for Women*,

Bedding Down: A Collection of Winter Erotica, and four editions of *The Mammoth Book of Best New Erotica*. She lives in Virginia with her husband, and they learned what it means to be "on island time" several years ago during a long, lusty weekend trip to Key West. Visit her—on island time or any time—at www.kristinawright.com.

ABOUT THE EDITOR

Called a "trollop with a laptop" by *East Bay Express*, a "literary siren" by Good Vibrations, and "over caffeinated" by her favorite local barista, **ALISON TYLER** has made being naughty a full-time job. Her sultry short stories have appeared in more than eighty anthologies including *Rubber Sex* (Cleis), *Dirty Girls* (Seal Press), and *Sex for America* (Harper Perennial). She is the author of more than twenty-five erotic novels, most recently *Melt With You* (Virgin), and the editor of more than forty-five explicit anthologies, including *J Is for Jealousy* (Cleis), *Naughty Fairy Tales from A to Z* (Plume), and *Naked Erotica* (Pretty Things Press).

Ms. Tyler is loyal to coffee (black), lipstick (red), and tequila (straight). She has tattoos, but no piercings; a wicked tongue, but a quick smile; and bittersweet memories, but no regrets. She believes it won't rain if she doesn't bring an umbrella, prefers hot and dry to cold and wet, and loves to spout her favorite motto: "You can sleep when you're dead." She chooses Led Zeppelin over the Beatles, the Cure over the Smiths, and the Stones over everyone—yet although she appreciates good rock, she has a pitiful weakness for '80s hair bands.

In all things important, she remains faithful to her partner of nearly fifteen years, but she still can't choose just one perfume.

Find her on the web 24/7 at www.alisontyler.com, or visit www.myspace.com/alisontyler if you want to be her friend.